THE KNACKERS

They came from outer space, these hideous, intelligent monsters, and they wanted our colonies, our goods, even our flesh. They looked like a cross between a spider and a crab, except bigger—much bigger—and meaner—much meaner—and they never stopped coming! World after world has been devastated, and man has been forced into a continuous defensive retreat.

Joel Karsh is just a grunt slugging it out on Planet 3G 789, a bug factory world, where fresh protein (*i.e.*, human flesh) is being processed for reshipment to enemy ships and depots throughout the Cluster. All he wants to do is make it back to the SpaceForce pick-up point. But as his buddies are killed, one by one, and the Knackers swarm ever closer, he's beginning to wonder if he'll even live through the next day!

A rousing SF military adventure by a master story-teller!

SLAUGHTER-HOUSE WORLD

A TALE OF THE HUMAN-KNACKER WAR

ARDATH MAYHAR

THE BORGO PRESS
MMX

SLAUGHTERHOUSE WORLD

FIRST EDITION

Published by Wildside Press LLC

www.wildsidebooks.com

DEDICATION

For Rob Reginald,

Who gave this unpublished tale a chance
After it had been languishing in the files for years

CONTENTS

PROLOGUE

I always loved science fiction and wrote quite a bit, though usually not what I call "gadgety" sf. This was one of the last pure sf stories I wrote. I've always thought it was fun, though it really needed to be turned into a full-length book, I think. Unfortunately, about that time things happened to turn off my "switch," and I never had the energy to expand it into a longer narrative. It's complete as it stands, however.

—Ardath Mayhar
Chireno, Texas
Nov., 2009

CHAPTER ONE

Joel held his breath as he watched Sergeant Gumble put one cautious foot onto the grass-patch and ease his weight down with great care. Once the noncom reassured himself that he had a foothold clear of any lurking dingballs, he knelt and ran his scanner over the entire plot, pinpointing the minute bits of instant death and pointing them out to the Tech carrying the Extractor.

"Gumboil's getting slower every day," one of the newer replacements grumbled.

The Tech corporal turned and glared. "You better be glad of it," he said, his voice grim. "I know men that've been in their graves for years, because their sergeant wasn't a stickler like Gumboil—Gumble," he corrected himself hastily.

"You might get by with a slacker back at HQ or with the desk-pushers on the third moon, but here you're dealing with the Knackers, and that is no game. Now shut your mouths and be glad of a chance to rest."

Joel said nothing. He had seen some of those men blown to bloody bits. More than once, he'd narrowly missed being one of those scattered to the winds of this hostile world. Now he just hunkered onto a patch of solid rock, obviously clear of antipersonnel devices, and waited, hoping hard that this was going to be one of the easy times. One of the good times...but he knew that was too much to wish for.

Around him, the craggy landscape rose, mostly rock, the cliff at the left scored with small runnels. Some of those had worn the stone from the heights into soil that lined their lower, flatter reaches.

If all had been solid granite, it would have been a snap. Unfortunately, the Knackers used those frequent grassy stretches, which led from the sheer cliffs to the Rift away to the east, for setting their nasty little traps.

He shifted his weight to the other heel and pulled out a twist of hard rations to chew while he waited. Stopping for a meal was something unknown in this particular war. Anyone who developed regular habits and thought he had to stick to them found himself dead before his first week was out. He'd seen a lot of those come and go.

The Forces had learned that, even before he had been conscripted from his shocked and frightened home world. They'd counted their losses from their first Knacker raid, panicked, and sent a hundred thousand young men and women to die for the glory of saving humankind from the Enemy.

He'd been skeptical, for a while, after he arrived on-planet. Then old "Gumboil" over there had led him into his first attack on a Knacker installation, and he had seen what was inside one of their processing plants. It still made him gag.

Knackers weren't human. Didn't even look human. Technically, they weren't cannibals, for that meant eating your own kind. But he had staggered after Gumble through a processing factory filled with men and women and children, in various stages of being skinned, butchered, cooked, and canned. He'd thought, for a while afterward, that he would never be able to eat anything out of a can again, especially pink meat.

That made you forget such nit-picking quibbles. As far as he was concerned, he was helping to make the Cosmos safe from cannibalism, and that was good enough for him.

Even as he thought that, there was a swift hissing. He flung himself flat behind the rock on which he had perched and covered his head with his arms. A muted explosion shook the ground, and he hugged it even more firmly.

Bits of reddish debris came spattering down among the platoon members, raining onto his back and neck. Joel wiped a red-stained hand against the big rock beside him, feeling his gorge rise in horror and disgust. No matter how many times you got a friend's guts blown all over you, it never got to be easy to handle.

He squinted through the dust and dead grass now drifting downward. It wasn't Gumboil who had been killed, he was grateful to find. But it was Greeley, and he had been a companion for a long time, as such things went on 3G 789. Six weeks was a lifetime friendship here.

He had an evil feeling that...yes, here it came.

"Karsh! Come up here and bring a spare Extractor. There must have been something wrong with that one. Sent Greeley all over the map."

Gumboil was covered with a dreadful sort of camouflage, done in shades of brown and red and mucus-gray. From his expression—what you could see of it—he might have been discussing the weather. Joel had been with the sergeant long enough to know that he would be sick for two days after the platoon managed to get back to the drop-point and up to Base, but for as long as the job took, Gumble would seem to be completely unaffected.

Joel swallowed bile and turned to Cleery, the supply corporal, who pulled the last spare Extractor out of its notch in the pack and handed it over with a sympathetic shrug. They had lost four Techs so far, and they had only been on patrol for two days.

When this Extractor went, they would be left with nothing to use to pull out the dingballs. That would mean either returning to base or risking their skins every time they tried crossing grass.

CHAPTER TWO

Well, it had been an interesting war. He'd lasted longer than he ever thought he would, and perhaps he had done some good. Probably not, of course, since the Knackers seemed never to be where they were expected and always appeared wherever the Rescue Force was least prepared to cope with them.

They raided worlds near the hub of the Cluster, taking people like cattle. They struck the Rim as well, always in an area considered safe, and took their captives, alive, back to this useless lump of rock, where they had set up their processing plants, without being detected for decades.

Their depredations spurred human interstellar warp technology to match their own superb capabilities. And that allowed the raided worlds to track them down and send troops after them. Not that they were doing much good, but at least they were trying.

Once the Force discovered that 3G 789 was the factory area for their activities, they struck the Knackers hard and often. The war so far had been a disaster, and Joel suspected that only the desperation of the situation kept the worlds sending their young people there to be ground up in its mill.

Nobody in his right mind could bear the thought of being eaten. Even less could he stand the idea of being canned for shipment to a world of Knackers, who considered human flesh a delicacy unparalleled in the universe.

Joel moved up carefully beside the sergeant, stepping only on the cleared patches. He looked down intently and knelt to wait for the signal to Extract. If they could cross this patch and two more, they could get into position to call down strikes from the third moon onto the Knacker position beyond the cliff.

He thought longingly of air drops, but the terrible up- and downdrafts forbade that method of putting men into position. More than one Lifter had been dashed to bits against the cliff or cast down into the Rift, never to rise again.

It seemed that nothing men had invented to use for warfare was quite suitable for use on the surface of this world. Only a strike from the moon, called down upon precise coordinates at exactly the right point in the satellite's transit, had proved devastating to the Knackers. Getting into position to report such coordinates had been fatal to thousands of his kind already.

He shook his head and kept his eyes on the Scanner. Gumboil was working steadily, calmly, without sign of nerves. He hadn't any, Joel had decided long before. Even his emotional spells after losing friends were controlled, as if he were purging himself of the pain.

Behind them, the lieutenant was chewing his moustache. Joel could hear the grit of hair between the boy's teeth. Without Gumboil, poor Harries would be in a bind, for this was his first assignment.

Gumble grunted, without words. Joel squinted through the finder and spotted the dingball trace that the Scanner had detected. He slid the Extractor beneath the wide flange of the instrument. It gave a quiet click, and the trace disappeared. One more dingball had been deactivated and discarded, now harmless.

They worked forward across the grass strip, making a pathway some meter and a half wide. Clearing more than that took too long; stringing the men out into a line was safer, in the long run.

They were within six yards of the rock beyond the strip when Joel turned his head. This was something he never did when working the Extractor, for he had noted, over the months of his tour, that those who lost their concentration usually lost their lives along with it.

But something compelled him, and he looked back across the strip, past the squatting men, toward the angle of the cliff around which they had come some hours before. Then he yelled. The platoon scrambled into crevices in the rock wall beside them, but it was too late.

The detachment of Knackers, sweeping along on their multiple limbs like an army of man-bodied spiders, were on them. They'd come straight down the cliffside, and it had been motion in that unusual place that caught the corner of Joel's eye.

The neurogas from their tubes enveloped the men in the cliff notches. Joel, without stopping to think, rose onto his toes and jumped as far as he could from a standing start.

For a wonder, he did not land on a dingball. Another spring took him almost to the edge of the grass and a third carried him beyond it.

He turned on his heel and stared back across the deadly patch. One figure was leaping wildly down the cleared path, past Gumble, who was stretched forward, his head on his arm as if he had fallen asleep. Cleery, the supply Corp, was coming to join him, his pack still on his back.

The corporal left the safe portion of the grass and leaped, as Joel had done, trying to land in the flattened grass of his tracks. Joel waited, though he knew he should be running, for the Knackers were milling around, trying to find all the bodies beyond the strip.

They never wasted any of their kills, that being the reason for the neurogas, which left the meat untainted. They wanted human flesh when it was freshly killed. Until they had secured the bodies back there, they would not trouble to follow two that were obviously doomed. They would keep, fresh and on the hoof, until the Knackers could catch up with them later.

Once Cleery was beside him, he turned and ran full out toward the next knee of cliff that jutted onto the stony flat. He could hear the Corp's breath panting along behind him, and it was a comfort to know that he wasn't completely alone.

He had no idea how they might survive or what they could do to find their way to the drop-point again, but he was alive, and that was something. Too many, back there, were dead.

CHAPTER THREE

They rounded the cliff at last, and Joel felt his lungs burning, his heart about to burst with effort and fear. Once out of eyeshot of the scene of slaughter, both paused to catch their breath, and Joel felt the scope of the disaster catching up with him. His fear was making him stink with its own desperate tang.

The anger was almost worse.

"We've got to do something," he said to Cleery. "They'll get us, sooner or later, but we can do them some damage, surely, if we think hard enough."

"Think?" Cleery's voice was thin with terror. "So you stand here and think at those man-eaters. I'm going to run and keep on running until...."

"They run you down and can you as Grade A Human Meat." Joel stared at him with all the anger that was in him. "So you get eaten anyway, and you're exhausted too. I intend to go someplace where they don't expect me."

He was thinking of those hairy feet at the ends of the multiple legs, clinging to the cliff as if it might be a flat road. They had supplementary arms too, with hook-like claws that could grasp the smoothest surface.

"We are going up. Straight up. And if you don't want to, you can try to outrun them, all by yourself. But I want half of what's in your pack. You won't need any of it, of course, once they catch you, but I couldn't take everything and feel right about it."

The Corp stared at him, his face greeny-white, his eyes dark and wild. But what he saw in Joel's face seemed to steady him a bit, and his breathing eased. He shrugged off the pack and put it on the rocky soil.

"You take what you want...unless...you really think we can get up that thing?" He stared up the cliff, which slanted slightly inward above them, obviously impossible to climb without specialized equipment or the sort of feet the Knackers had.

"I'm going up. If those creatures can do it, I can figure out a way to. And they're never going to think we went up, because nobody ever has tried out-climbing them before. Not and lived to tell about it." Joel was already shifting part of the contents of the pack into his own gear, so as to lighten Cleery's load.

He tucked the Extractor back into its notch. They might find their lives depending on that tool, before everything was over. It was light enough not to matter, though now both packs were a bit bulkier than was comfortable on such a difficult climb.

It was late afternoon. There was a good chance they could move up to some ledge that would give them a place to stop before it became totally dark. If the Knackers finished harvesting their kill back there in time to come after them before the sun went down, it would be that much harder for them to see anyone high up the cliffside. Everything told Joel to start at once and not to stop until he had to.

"Come on," he said to Cleery. "Put your hands and feet where you see mine go, if you can. Ever done any rock climbing?"

"Scared of heights," Cleery said. He sounded resigned, which was better than desperate, Joel hoped fervently.

The cliff was sheer, but it was weathered and broken into cracks and crannies by the severe winters and the harsh summers of this uninviting world. He found he could manage to jam a toe here, a finger there, enough to begin inching his way upward.

From time to time, he found himself stuck, with seemingly no place to go. This put Cleery, below him, into a bind, for he would have to go back down in order to let Joel backtrack to find another route.

His fingers went numb, of course, and also began bleeding, but the thought of hungry Knackers coming along the path below kept him at it. Before the sky grew entirely dark, he located a narrow slot, extending to left and right for a considerable distance, into which he could push himself.

He called down softly to Cleery, "Found something. If it's as deep as it looks, we can both fit into it. If not, half of each of us can go in, and we won't sleep much. Keep coming before it gets too dark to see. I'm going in to see what we have here."

There came a muffled grunt from below, and he

knew the Corp was still climbing, frightened as he must be. Joel reached into the slot, searching for a handhold that would make it easy to pull himself in. It was smooth and gritty, like the rest of the cliff. He sighed and worked his right leg upward, straining to keep his weight on the toe precariously tucked into a cranny in the rock face.

When his foot cleared the edge, he sighed with relief...just as the other boot slipped free from its hold. But he had both hands and a foot still over the rim of the ledge, and it was enough.

He heaved himself inside, lying flat and feeling the cold stone above him against his back as he slithered forward up the crack, feeling before him with both hands.

Something ahead of him hissed. Not a reptile—they had found none on this ball of rock—but something with a nasty temper. He stopped and worked a hand back down past his hip to the pack, which was dangling along down the side of the drop. He found the halogen torch, tiny and long-lasting, and twisted the rim.

Raw white light blazed down the cranny, and four scarlet eyes glared at him from an even narrower crack leading deeper into the cliff. He scrabbled together a handful of grit and flung it awkwardly toward the creatures, whatever they might be.

There came a hissing snarl, and the eyes disappeared. Creatures small enough to fit into that space couldn't be dangerous, unless they had poison teeth, he decided. But he kept the torch in his leading hand, lighting his way forward.

The notch grew no taller, but it did widen a bit, so he could pull up his pack to slide along beside him. He heard Cleery trying to make it into the crevice and called back, "Get a foot in, Corp. Then if the other one goes, you'll be in good shape."

A growl and a couple of groans answered him, but he heard the unmistakable sounds of someone bellying along behind him and knew his companion had made it safely. He sighed, realizing for the first time that he had been holding his breath while Cleery climbed.

The crack was very long, not very wide, and extremely shallow. Once he was on his face, as he had to be to crawl, there was no turning over without going out onto the face of the cliff again to reorient himself. It was going to get very old, lying with his face in the grit all night.

Then he thought of spending the night in one of the Knackers' processing plants, and the hard ledge seemed suddenly far more comfortable.

When Cleery reached to tap his boot-heel, he said, "Well, Corp, looks as if we lucked out, this time. We have all the comforts of home...no Knackers. No cleavers and knives. No canning vats. But we're not going to be turning over in our sleep. I hope you're going to be able to rest."

Cleery spat. Joel heard the wad hit the rock on the cliff side. "Better than where we were," he said. "I can sleep on a rock. In fact, I intend to." And he said no more.

After a while, Joel heard a rumbling snore, and he closed his eyes hastily. If he didn't doze off quickly, the echoes of the corporal's nightly snorts would keep him awake, no matter how tired he might be.

CHAPTER FOUR

Light sifting into the slot waked him. The cliff carried sound upward very efficiently, and he heard skittering footsteps that had to be made by the Knackers' many legs and hairy feet on the gritty rock below.

There was a blur of talk in their staccato tongue, and he noted with satisfaction that they seemed puzzled. They milled around for some time, and he heard several instances that he would have sworn were arguments between conflicting views.

"Sarge, those varmints can't go up; they got to run on the flat. If we just keep going, then we're bound to catch up with them!" he imagined the deepest set of jabbers to be saying.

Then, "The tracks don't go on. They don't go back. They don't cut away toward the Rift. So they had to go up!" That would be the sergeant, or whatever the Knacker equivalent might be, livid with anger at the escape of two more gourmet menus.

He edged deeper into the slot, wedging his shoulder and hip as tightly as could be done. Behind him, he heard Cleery doing the same. Something ran across his outstretched hand, and he had to endure it, for he couldn't snatch it back.

Then he saw a long, thick animal, shaped something like a snake yet covered with fur, on the edge of the cut, staring down the cliff. Its fur bristled as if in irritation.

There was the sound of scritching against the cliff-side. The Knackers were coming up...and there was nothing whatever he could do about it. His weapon was in the pack, but even if he worked it out, there was no room to activate it. The blowback of the blast would roast him and Cleery, even if he managed to fire it. He sighed and dropped his face into the grit again.

A smell wafted into the crack, almost making him sneeze, for the Knackers had a dry and acrid odor. He held his breath, pushed his nose tightly against the stone, and almost blew his eardrums out with the confined pressure. They were almost up to the level of the ledge.

The fursnake snarled and hissed, and three more crossed his hand to join it. Evidently they had more company than they wanted or needed. Their weasel-like heads thrust out over the edge into the dawn light, and he could see that they had tube-like fangs, revealed when they made their ferocious hisses. He hoped he would never learn what sort of poison those fangs might inject.

The scritching stopped. There came a sudden jabber from just below his position, as well as from the bottom of the cliff. That other voice was muted with distance. Now they were arguing about something again. Was this tiny creature something that even the Knackers feared? Again he imagined a conversation.

"There's no way they could have got up here. There's a bunch of whatsits in a crack, and you know they'd bite anything that came along."

"Check it out, anyway. You never know about animals, either these nasty little ones or those big tasty ones."

"But if I keep going, they're going to bite me, and that'll kill me. You won't be any better off, and I'll be a lot worse off!"

Whether or not that was what the gabble of talk meant, the scritching feet retreated down the cliff. Joel found that he had pissed his pants. Behind him, he heard a soft curse from Cleery, and he suspected the same thing had happened to him.

They waited for a long time, while the sun reached its early rays into their hiding place, before rising farther and withdrawing them again. There came a few sounds of passing Knackers from below, but in time all indication of activity stopped.

Only the fursnakes moved about the cranny, slithering over and around the recumbent men in an irritated manner, yet without biting or even snarling.

When the chronometer on his outstretched wrist had counted off three hours, Joel said, "Cleery, we'd better get moving. We want to reach the top of this thing before they decide to take another look around for us."

Cleery snorted. "Fine with me. I'm lying here in my own piss, cramped to the point of no return. Anything's better, even that triple-cursed cliff."

It wasn't easy to find a spot where there was enough of a handhold to haul himself out of the crack. When Joel found himself, at last, half out of the notch, holding to a bulge of rock with both hands and staring about for a route, he found they had climbed much higher than he thought.

There were only a dozen yards more above them, and the jagged top of the escarpment seemed within reach, without too much danger. He inched along on his butt, fingering for notches that would let him climb again, not to mention allowing Cleery to survive the venture out onto the rock face.

At last he reached a narrow chimney—more than he had ever dared to hope for, and managed to work his way into a semi-vertical position.

"This is going to be a piece of cake," he called quietly to his companion. "Watch where I am and come out right here. You can see my drag-tracks in the grit."

Cleery grunted, his tone skeptical. He might make a rock-climber yet.

CHAPTER FIVE

Before noon, they were on the top. They looked like remnants from a particularly dirty battle, cut and bloody and dirty, but they were alive. They also had the supply pack and their weapons.

Joel lay flat above a camp teeming with Knackers, who were so far below they seemed like ants, as they went about their orderly business of moving item A to spot B, or vice versa.

Joel could make nothing of their activity, except to note with relief that no human beings seemed to be involved. From time to time, one of their roller-tracked vehicles would come out of a hole in the side of the mountain and load itself, before disappearing again into the subterranean mysteries from which it had come.

They were creating a big-time base there, invisible from the moons, even with enhanced scanners. Once all those piles of equipment and masses of Knackers were out of the valley where they worked, nothing would be visible from above, no matter how closely it was observed.

"You still have that Com unit?" he asked Cleery,

who looked insulted at the question.

The corporal sat behind the upthrust of rock sheltering them from observation from below and pulled the flexible antenna out of the seam of the pack. The squat unit, the size of a fist, came to life at once, when the sunlight touched the uncovered cell in its housing, and the antenna's addition brought its signal to a hum.

Joel squatted beside Cleery, as the corporal tapped out their message on the key set into the Com's side. Human beings had found it impossible to conceal their most sophisticated transmissions from the Knackers' sensitive detectors. Only the old Morse code, spark-activated, had proved to be safe for use on this world. The Knackers, as far as anyone knew, had no clue to the code, even if they happened onto the signal, which to those beings was completely alien.

Their coordinates went through, together with information about and coordinates of the new Knacker base, followed by a brief report on the engagement of the afternoon before. Cleery tapped:

REQUEST FURTHER INSTRUCTIONS FOR CORPORAL CLEERY AND TECH KARSH. PRESENTLY ON CLIFF TOP ABOVE TARGET. VERY DANGEROUS POSITION, WHEN ATTACK BEGINS. REPEAT. REQUEST ORDERS.

The Com hummed for a long moment. Then the light set into its housing began to blink, short and long, in Morse:

CALIBRATIONS SET. ATTACK TO BE-
GIN FIFTEEN HUNDRED HOURS. TAKE
SHELTER. TAKE SHELTER. WAIT FOR
ORDERS. OUT.

And that was it. Joel stared down at his boots, and he heard Cleery's curses with sympathy. They were alive. They could go back down the cliff and stash themselves in that cranny with the fursnakes.

They could even, he thought, quite possibly make it back to the pickup point for Base, once the Knackers were sorting out their own disaster. But it wasn't what he had hoped for, and that was a fact.

With a sigh, he began reeling the antenna back into the seam of the pack, while Cleery put the Com into its padded section. Fifteen hundred hours—that gave them about an hour and a half to get back down to their hidey-hole. And then?

He started down the steep, feeling with toes, gripping with fingers, trying to forget those fangs the fursnakes showed when they hissed. He hoped the little beasts would be gladder to see him than he would be to see them.

"Steady on," he said to Cleery, now above his head and pattering grit down onto his shoulders. "We'll make it fine, Corp."

Cleery's reply was profane but oddly cheerful.

Joel felt again with a foot, reached with a battered hand and went on again with his duty. They were safe enough for now. After what had already happened, getting back to the drop-point through a bunch of angry Knackers seemed almost easy, and there just might be a bit of damage they could do along the way.

Below, a fursnake hissed, but he found himself strangely untroubled by the sound. In a bit, that particular Knacker installation was going to go up in smoke.

There was only one place they could reach in time, without running the risk of meeting Knackers. The slot with the fursnakes had to be it, Joel decided, with considerable reluctance.

Cleery, clinging to the rock like a panicky lizard, crawled into the crack after him. Once more they found themselves waiting, cramped and chilled, for what might come next.

The hissing of the creatures about them sounded fretful, but again they slid over and around the intruders without biting. On the contrary, they seemed relatively undisturbed by the presence of the men.

Joel wondered if there was something about the Knacker scent that particularly irritated the things, for they had certainly not been happy at the approach of the Knacker climber the night before. That acrid tang—it just might be one the creatures couldn't endure.

But there was no way to solve that problem or any other. His task was to wait and then to find a way along the river back to the drop.

To his intense disgust, Cleery began snoring cheerfully: the man truly had no nerves. Gumble had controlled his feelings, but except for a short time before beginning their climb, Cleery had shown no sign of discomfort whatsoever. Joel envied him.

CHAPTER SIX

He closed his eyes, but instead of growing drowsy he found himself remembering his home on Gyrfalcon. He had thought his work as a landscaper the most boring employment known to man. Now he would have given much to be back in the Long Garden at the Statehouse, planting abelias and Permesian roses and pulling out purple-weeds.

His thirst for adventure had been pretty well quenched, but there was no way now to return to his former life. He knew from his months of service that only those returning as ashes to the Sleep-Gardens of their kin went back before their terms of conscription were up.

He had a suspicion that some of those who had deserted early in his time on this ugly world had been dropped deliberately into the paths of Knackers. They probably were, even now, sitting in containers on their way to the Knacker worlds.

He must have dozed, for he dreamed of Venna. It seemed she was there with him in that cranny, waiting for the strike, when the third moon reached the proper spot in the sky. She was moving with her usual sureness through the garden ahead of him, pointing out the places where plants must go in or come out.

The Herbarium, which was her own particular responsibility, loomed ahead of her, and as she reached its circular hatch she turned and looked into his eyes. "You be careful, Joel. This isn't a picnic you're going to, and I want you back in one piece. We've got a farm we want to buy with the money we're going to save from your danger bonus and my pay, so keep that in mind." Her weather-beaten face was glowing with color, and her eyes shone dark and compelling.

He yearned with sudden intensity to be with her on their farm, perhaps with children growing up and his parents coming to visit. Then he woke, as the rock beneath him shuddered.

The fursnakes began rustling about him, hissing and complaining and rubbing their plushy sides against him as if for comfort. Cleery snorted and coughed.

"Karsh, I think they've begun," he yelled, above the creaking and crackling of the stone and the deep reverberations from the distant explosions. "And I think they're giving the Knackers back a bit of what they've been dealin' out for so long."

Joel hugged the rock and found the soft touch of a fursnake against his neck strangely pleasant. Anything alive was good, in the middle of this bedlam of destruction and death. He felt the small one against his side pushing its triangular face into one of the pockets of his Combats. It slid into the space, tight against his leg, and lay there, shivering.

"I think the fursnakes are scared to death!" he roared, but now the noise was so great Cleery didn't hear him. There was nothing in all the universe except the tumult that rang and rattled and shuddered through the stone, shaking down pebbles about his ears, sending slabs of rock thundering down the cliffside. What it must be like in that cupped valley where the Knackers worked he didn't like to think. Even a Knacker was to be pitied in such a situation.

Even when the bombardment stopped, the crackle of splitting formations, seething from the intensity of the energy beams, still sounded through the cliff. The beam cannon heated anything in its path to incandescence, and metal ran, rock melted or split and crumbled. Flesh, Joel knew too well, disappeared with a stink and a bit of greasy smoke. Teeth sometimes survived to rain down on the smoking soil.

He had turned the dreadful nozzle of one of the field versions on a troop of Knackers once. And, far worse, he had been on a hilltop directing fire when a troop of the Force had been caught by accident in its path. He hated thinking about that, and he tried to turn his mind away, grinding his nose into the grit and stopping his ears with two fingers.

The cliff seemed to rock for a long time after the worst of the tumult died away. Half deafened, he was able, at last, to hear the hissing of the furry creatures huddled about his length, pressing their long bodies against his.

Cleery spoke through a series of sneezes. "Never—

choo!—thought I'd like to—choo!—have these little buggers around. Kind of nice, now. Ahhhh-choo!"

Joel agreed. He wriggled sideways and peered out of the slit into space. Dust was thick, and the sun was now down behind the mountains, but he could see dimly. The flat ground below the cliffs was invisible in the thickness, but the stark line of the Rift, there where the river had cut its path for thousands of years at the foot of the anticline, showed black against the paler cliffs beyond it.

"We'd better shift, while we can see how to climb down," he said. "If there are any Knackers ranging the low country, they're going to come swarming up here to see what has happened to their buddies."

"Think I'll take a couple of our own buddies with me," said Cleery. "You 'member how they hissed at them Knackers tried to climb up here? They might just be a sort of Knacker early warning system. You think?"

Joel felt the furry shapes, now relaxed up and down his sides and even on his back. There was no threat in them—not to his kind, it was obvious. But the Knackers were afraid of them, he was sure. Or else why hadn't that climber kept coming right on up and found its quarry?

"That's a good idea, Corp," he said. "Though if they object to going with us, I'm not about to quarrel with them about it. Let's see what happens to the ones in my pockets, when I start to move. That should tell the tale."

He moved sideways and forward. Then he felt along the edge, searching for a handhold that would let him make his way out onto the face. The creature in his pocket lay quietly, not even wriggling when he pinched it against the rock, though he worried about that more than a bit.

Then he was out on the cliff-face, clinging to the scanty hand and footholds, as Cleery came after him and put his head out of the slot that had sheltered them. Blindly, he felt downward with a searching toe, found a crack, and moved out of Cleery's way.

It was far worse going down than it had been coming up. Before, he had seen where he was going. Now every movement was a risk, for he never knew if the foothold he found would hold him. Several times, rotten stone crumbled beneath his toe, and only the desperate grip of his fingers on knobs or in crannies kept him from plunging to his death.

Cleery, above him, was in better shape, for Joel directed his downward steps, watching until his feet were securely placed.

It took hours of desperate effort, and twice they had to retrace their route to find a passable way. But at last both stood on the gravel at the foot of the cliff, staring up at the sheer wall down which they had come.

"Think they got the base?" Cleery asked. He sneezed again.

"I hope they got the base," Joel said. "What do you say, Corp? Which way do we go? I think there may be Knackers swarming over this area before long."

Cleery stared at him. "Karsh, I'm no brain. I'm a supply corporal, and a damn good one, but I don't give orders and I don't figure out answers to tough questions. Gumble used to tell me if I had a brain I'd lose it down a mouse hole. So I'll make a deal with you.

"You do the thinking. I'll back you up in anything you decide to do, and if we get back to the Drop I'll take the blame for anything that goes wrong. How's that?"

Joel smiled. "Fine with me, Corp. I suggest we get the hell out of here right now. I feel that's the safest thing to do—*right now.*"

Without the Extractor, that would have been impossible to accomplish. They angled toward the river, avoiding the grassy strips as much as they could, but from time to time there were places where runnels had carried away the soil in a maze of long ribbons of dirt, all of which were covered with growth.

The Knackers scattered dingballs everywhere there was concealment—Joel thought they must drop them every time they took to the shuttles to reach their own mother ship. The Scanner was gone with Gumble, but the smaller one set into the Extractor was enough to allow them to find those in their direct path.

They moved with glacial slowness, but in the darkness that came down on the flatland they could not risk speed. At least, out there in the open as they were, the darkness hid them from anything except a scanner that spotted life-forms.

The dust and smoke in the air had thinned to a haze

when the second moon rose. That made a muddy light by which Joel could see a bit deeper into the gloom than before. When the fursnake in his side pocket began hissing like a leaking valve, that light allowed him to see the Knacker group before its members could see him and Cleery.

A half dozen of the leggy creatures were stalking along between the escarpment and the Rift, their gait swift and their attention obviously focused on the catastrophe ahead of them in the mountains. Joel sank flat and Cleery beat him down.

The fursnakes subsided into a faint sibilance. Those in his pockets again seemed comforted by the size and warmth of his body. He wondered what, aside from general irritation, the Knackers had done to make themselves so roundly hated by the cliff-dwellers.

However, the hostility was proving useful, and he welcomed the furry shapes in his pockets as he heard the group clack and scritch away into the night. Whoever is my enemy's enemy is my friend, he remembered reading in some long-forgotten book.

Perhaps he and Cleery had found allies, here on the Knackers' slaughterhouse world.

CHAPTER SEVEN

Within the space of that night, the countryside began to crawl with Knackers. Only the discovery of a deep cleft, too narrow to be visible from below, in one of the buttress cliffs allowed Joel and Cleery to escape discovery many times over.

That climb was one Joel never remembered long afterward, for he scampered up the steep with the sounds of Knacker claws clicking in his ears from below. The fursnakes in his pockets were hissing like small kettles all the way, though they quieted when he reached the ledge. That became, in time, another slot into which he and Cleery crammed themselves.

"You were right," Joel said, wiping grit from his face onto his wrist. "These creatures make fine warning systems. If they all hadn't gone off like raid alarms, we would have been, if you'll pardon the pun, in the soup."

The Corp snorted. "If you'd of told me, before, that I'd be carryin' around a bunch of little furry animals, I'd of said you were crazy. But here we are, and we seem to be getting farther from the river, instead of closer to it. How in hell we going to make it to the Drop if we can't get down into the Rift? If the Knackers don't get us, the dingballs will, and you and I both know it."

Joel stared out into the dawn. The distant lowland was astir with spider-legged shapes, which hurried about their search with a determination that didn't reassure him at all.

"We just got to lie here and eat grit and wait," he said. "If they were going to find us up here, I think they already would've. That bunch we almost ran into was too close to miss getting us on their scanners. The only thing that may have saved us, besides going straight up the cliff again, was having the life-traces of the fursnakes all mixed up with ours.

"We must have a dozen or more inside our clothes and in our pockets, and that makes a pretty good amount of alien trace. Maybe their equipment can't untangle it and thinks this is some new kind of life entirely." The thought comforted him considerably.

However it was, there seemed no interest among the searchers in climbing any of the cliffs walling the west side of the valley that ended at the Rift. As the shadows crept eastward, the search moved away northward, leaving the lowland quiet and colorless.

The first moon was a fleck of silver light just above the horizon beyond the Rift, now. Soon darkness covered the country below them, and no further sound of Knacker equipment or personnel came to Joel's ears. It was time to move, if they were ever going to get clear of the escarpment.

He poked Cleery with an elbow. "Wake up, Corp. Time to shag our asses out of here."

The corporal groaned. Then he spat out the gravel that had found its way into his mouth while he dozed, face-down, on the ledge. "If I'd of known how much dirt I was goin' to eat on this tour of duty, I'd of took my discharge and never re-upped. Knackers I can stand, at a distance and for a little while, but grit in my teeth just about makes my hide crawl clean off me." His tone of disgust was one that Joel knew of old.

"Grit or no grit, we've got to move," he said. "And maybe down below we can make enough time to get to the river. Thank God the water's good!"

The long stretch of flat ground looked deceptively peaceful, under the light of the small moon. There was very little of that sort of terrain on 3G 789, and Joel found himself particularly wary of this one. He'd already had enough experience with the nasty little matters that could be found in innocent-looking places.

Cleery, behind him, cleared his throat. "You think we can risk it?" he asked. "Or is it just too good to be true?"

Sitting on his heels in the shelter of a squatty tree with more thorns than leaves, Joel surveyed the expanse. He remembered with great clarity the other Techs who had been blown to confetti by the dingballs set in the grassy strips. The fact that only the pair of them was left alive and unprocessed by the Knackers was enough to make him think a long while before risking anything at all.

He caught a hint of motion at the corner of his eye that made him freeze in the stringy shadow of the tree.

Cleery grunted softly too. Then they waited, patient as primitives, to see what was traveling across the stony stretch flanking this segment of the mountain chain.

There was no sense in retracing the route the platoon had taken. That was probably going to be swarming with Knackers, furious from the earlier attacks against their stronghold, for days to come. Yet Joel knew that he and Cleery had to get back upriver to find the drop area. Only there could the shuttle pick them up. Only then would they find any safety on this world.

There was another flicker of motion, moonlight flashing on something pale, which seemed to be crawling over the rough ground, moving away from the dark line that marked the edge of the cleft holding the river. Joel heard Cleery getting the Glass from his pack.

"By Gerroun and Gannesaw!" the older man grunted. "Look, Karsh. Just you look what's escaped from the Knackers."

Joel reached back for the Glass, which had been adjusted to its infra-red mode. Setting the eyepiece in place, he scanned the weird contrasts of the area ahead, found a strong impulse, and realized he was looking at a woman.

CHAPTER EIGHT

She was, of course, strange-looking in this mode, but it was a real live human woman. She wasn't in combats, so she had to be one of the "cattle" the Knackers had brought here for the slaughter. That posed an entire set of new problems.

Before, they had only had to worry about getting to the drop-site. Now they had to worry about whether or not to try getting this totally unexpected civilian out with them. Cleery was already skinning out of his pack, getting ready to head for the rescue.

"Corp," said Joel, his tone carefully non-aggressive, "don't you think you ought to check this out a little more before you go dashing out there in the open?"

"Shut up!" the corporal growled, his tone fierce. "The day ain't come when I'll sit by and let a human woman get eaten by a bunch of hairy-legged Knackers, without doing something to stop it. You sit here until your ass falls off. I'm going out there and fetch her in."

Joel felt perfectly sympathetic, but something about the set-up made his neck-hair crawl. This was just too plain and easy-seeming. First of all, nobody he'd ever heard about had escaped from the Knackers. They were all shot full of dope that kept them barely ambulatory, if you could believe the Intelligence reports. Their minds were shut off, and just their bodies worked. So if there was a real human woman out there in the thin veil of moonlight, it was just about certain that she had been put there by her captors.

"Listen!" Joel insisted.

Cleery paused, his back still to the Tech. "To what?" he asked.

"How do you suppose anybody could get loose from the aliens, let alone get out of one of those cattle pens they keep their...their live catch in?"

"People can get out of anything, you give them a chance," the corporal said. He sounded irritated.

"And nothing about this set-up smells to you like a trap?" Joel was trying to sound perfectly cool. "I want to go and get her too, but what I don't want is to go rushing out there like some damned Holovee actor and get myself caught.

"They've got to know that somebody out of our platoon survived. Hell, they tracked us. Then we called down the missile strike on that stronghold—they're not stupid, Cleery. They know somebody is loose on old ThreeGee, and what better way would there be to get us than to trick us into doing something crazy? Like rescuing a Fair Maiden in the middle of a rock-patch?"

"Tech Karsh, you can sit there, safe and snug under that thorn tree, until your teeth fall out. You can argue with that rock there. But you're not going to talk me out of going after that poor kid. She's scared to death—you just look through the Glass again, if you don't believe me. I've got a girl not much younger than she is— or I had one, till the triple-damned Knackers raided Terminus Two. I'm going!" He lay flat on his belly and began wriggling across the stony soil toward the river.

Joel sighed. He would have liked to follow, but if there was chicanery afoot he would be needed here, with his weapon ready. Cleery was a good supply corporal, but he never claimed to be a Big Brain, much less a tactician. If he was going to come out with his butt intact, he'd better have some backup.

Their Combats blended with almost anything. Even knowing that he was out there in the moonlight, not ten meters ahead of him, Joel found it hard to focus on the camouflage pattern, as the corporal moved. He kept his eyes flicking from side to side, scanning the distant shape of the woman, the dark side of the mountain to right and to left, the detail of the moonlit landscape, which was stark gray-black, hiding anything concealed in a shadow.

He used the Glass from time to time, hoping to pick up traces of any large living creature, but he hadn't much hope of that. The Knackers had learned to make some kind of material that shielded their images. Knowing their blood was considerably cooler than his own kind's, Joel felt sure it hadn't been as difficult as it sounded.

He looked at the woman again. Her face was a silvery triangle amid the mingled grays of the scraggly growth through which she crawled. Her eyes were wide, dark, terrified.

He felt sick with empathy, for a moment, thinking of what she must have gone through. As he watched, she saw Cleery at last. She went still for a moment.

Then she got to her feet and waved frantically. "Run! Run!" she shouted, her voice a tiny sound in the distance.

Cleery flattened himself, which was his superb instinct showing itself once again. A sear of energy flashed over the area, blinding Joel temporarily.

He fired off his own weapon in a sweeping beam of energy, knowing that Cleery and the girl had both gone down, dead or alive. By the time his eyes cleared, nothing was moving out in the open space.

Nothing moved into the moonlight to check on either of the people there. Evidently, incinerated flesh wasn't on the Knacker menu.

CHAPTER NINE

Joel waited until the shadow of the mountains at his back had covered half the span of grass. Then he slid out from his new position (nobody but a fool would have stayed in the spot from which he had fired), and began crawling toward the last spot in which he had seen Cleery. He went with care, as silently as possible, pausing from time to time to check out the terrain.

He put his hand on Cleery's foot, before he knew he had reached the corporal. The foot jerked. "Who's that?" came the gruff query.

"Karsh. You all right, Corp?"

"Alive. Scorched down my back, but nothing that won't get better, given the chance. You go and check out that little girl. She done her best to save me. I don't know if they got her or not. Haven't heard a thing, all this time."

He sighed heavily. "You're a good man, Karsh. If you'd come with me, we'd both be scorched, and maybe none of us would get out. You go on now. Check her out."

"Yessir." Joel grinned. Between Cleery's instinct and his own ability to think things out, they might just get out of this disaster alive. Too many of their comrades hadn't, that was certain.

He oriented himself by the calibrations he had set into the Glass, every time he had scanned the area. She should be off to his left, some twelve degrees. He flattened himself, shivered when he left the inky shadow, and slid over the sharp pebbles.

She, being clad in a pale coverall, was much easier to see than had been Cleery and the Combats he wore. She lay on her face, her head on her wrist. Her back quivered, and he knew with relief mixed with exasperation that she was alive.

"Hey!" he called softly. "You all right?"

The pale face lifted off the wrist. Dark eyes assessed him intently, as if she didn't dare trust in his appearance. Then she nodded.

"I think so, except for my back. They swept the beam over me very low, and it blistered me from neck to heels. But nothing serious, I think. How are we going to get out of this?"

Joel found he had other, more pressing questions, but this was not the time or the place to interrogate her. "Crawl after me. Keep your butt down—it's sticking up like a lump!" Without waiting, he turned and moved back toward Cleery.

The corporal had already retreated deep into the shadow of the range of peaks, and they found him picking bits of scorched material out of the blisters he could reach. Joel dug out the burn cream, a necessary item in every soldier's pack, and a few squirts made him more comfortable.

Diffidently, Joel asked the woman, "You want me to put some of this on your back? It'll help a lot. I think your burns are where you can't reach 'em very well, from the look of that coverall."

Cleery snorted and turned it into a cough. Cover-nothing would have been a better description of the garment the Knackers put on their waiting meat animals. It was a sort of cape wrapped over one shoulder and under the other, stamped with a symbol that was probably a number. About her waist was a strip of papery stuff, extending over her buttocks—barely—and marked off with directions for butchering this piece of meat.

The beam that seared the back had, of course, cut each piece into two, and it was with much difficulty that she was keeping something covering her front.

But she was a sensible girl, whatever it was that her instincts were telling her to do. Joel thought he would probably be screaming and crying, but she had set her teeth.

She nodded. "If you don't mind, that would help. It's getting painful, now the shock is wearing off a bit."

He dabbed his fingers into the stuff and stroked it onto her pale skin, forcing himself to think of some-thing other than how long it had been since he had seen his fiancée. It was hard to do.

"We go downriver," said Joel. "How, I don't yet know. But that is where the drop-point is."

He made it no more specific than that. If she had

been bugged by her captors, she wouldn't know it, of course, and that would tell the Knackers nothing they didn't already know. If she wasn't, there was no need to worry her with the difficulties of going where they had to go.

"How in 'ell did you get loose from those buggers?" asked Cleery. "I never knew nobody to do that before."

"I didn't. I didn't even know where I was or what was happening. They got me in my front yard, watering my roses"—she struggled to hold back tears. "When I came to, I was on a hard table in some kind of metal room, and these...well, I knew the Knackers were ugly and mean-tempered, but now I know how big an understatement that is.

"They were giving me some sort of shots. After a while I could sit up and think straight." She huddled her arms across the thin stuff covering her chest and shivered.

Joel reached into his pack and pulled out his blanket, which she accepted with a smile. Wrapping it about her, she went on. "They took me out in some kind of vehicle that moved on land and water both. They put me in the middle of that place and left me there.

"I didn't figure out what they were doing until I saw somebody crawling toward me. Then I knew it had to be a trap, and anybody they wanted to catch or kill had to be a friend of mine. So I yelled."

"They're out there, waiting for us to make another move," Cleery said. "And here we sit, pinned down neat as a bunch of fish in a pond. I didn't do you a bit of good, Miss...."

"Call me Helen," she said. "And I don't think we're pinned down. When they fired at you, I went down to keep out of the way. I was looking back at the spot where they'd hidden the weapon when this man fired back. He destroyed it and the Knacker they left to use it. I saw him go into the river, and the gun just...just melted. It's there now."

"No way they'd leave just one to clean us up," Cleery objected. "There've got to be more."

Joel was scanning with the Glass, back and forth, up and down. He could see bright flickers where insects' tiny lives speckled the meadow and the rock behind them. But there was nothing larger there.

He looked up at the two. "I think she's right. I got out there, and you both came back here, but nothing shot at us, nothing moved, nothing showed a bit of interest. *Think*, Cleery. Do we expect cattle or poultry to outsmart us? Sure as hell, we don't. They're meat animals, nothing else. If one does seem to out-think us, once in a while, we just put it down to accident and go on as usual."

Cleery grunted skeptically.

"Well, you just consider that. We outsmarted them once, but they must have thought it was a fluke. They put out bait, the way we used to spray pheromones to trap insects. Why should they leave more than one of their valuable personnel to operate the spray-gun?"

There was a long time of silence. Joel rethought his logic, and it still made sense to him. One Knacker to handle one problem with the enemy—who had it been, back on Old Earth, who had such a rule? Somebody tough, he seemed to recall.

Cleery spat. "Looks as if you might be right. And if so, once the shadow gets clean to the river we just might be able to dash across the flat and make it to the Rift. Then we could climb down to the water. We got up and down those cliffs, so we ought to be able to handle the Rift, don't you think?"

"I do. And once we make it to the water, there ought to be a reasonably good way to travel downstream without either getting caught or drowning. Or both," said Joel. "You game?" He glanced at Helen, who was sitting with both hands clasped around her knees, the tattered blanket pulled about her closely.

"I am game for anything whatsoever," she said, very clearly. "I prefer drowning to what I saw them doing to people, as they took me out of that Knacker factory. Shoot me if they catch us. Promise me that."

Joel, in his turn, grunted. "We'll all shoot each other," he said. "I don't care to die the death they'd give us. And I sure as hell don't intend to make an entrée for some fancy Knacker meal."

He sagged against a boulder, watching the moonlit space grow narrower and narrower, the shadows of the mountains encroach upon the edge of the Rift. It looked as if, just maybe, they might make it out of this mess yet.

CHAPTER TEN

They made it to the Rift before dawn, working their way with painful care across the valley, using every scrap of cover, every rock, every ridge or rut that broke the contour of the land. When Joel found himself staring down the drop to the river, he wondered for a stunned instant if it had all been a terrible waste. He had seen this world from space, and the distance had seemed not much greater than this titanic declivity.

The second moon was overhead, and the sky was already paling. That allowed him to see much farther down into the Rift than he liked. The stone of the wall was granite, grooved by the rains of runoff from the valley at his back. The river below was a silver thread. If anyone fell—he sighed, thinking of that terrible drop. Then he thought of the Knackers and realized it would be a kinder death than any alternative they could hope for.

When Cleery and Helen joined him at the edge, he heard their twin gasps. "Here we use a rope," he said. "I hope you still have some in your pack, Corp."

Cleery opened his worn pack and rummaged for a length of the tough line issued to the troops. "'Bout a thousand meters here," he said. He glanced down again, shuddered, and said, "Maybe more, but it's hard to tell in this light."

"We'd better wait for full daylight before we try," Karsh said. "Nobody is going to look for us down there, I think. We can't risk missing a hold because it's too dark to see."

Cleery grunted agreement. Joel reached into his pocket and felt the furry body of a fursnake. "You want to risk that drop?" he asked the slender shape as he drew the animal out into the growing dawnlight. "If you don't, I think you can make it on that cliff. There's probably some of your kin down there. It looks like your sort of place."

Helen, beside him, stared at the creature, her eyes wide. "What on earth is that?"

"It's not on Earth. I call it a fursnake, and we have several of them with us, in pockets and down backs. They're warm at night, and they hate Knackers. Hiss like teakettles when they sense any within whatever their range may be. Handy little buggers to have around."

She reached a timid finger and smoothed the ruffled fur. The snake seemed to coil upward against the touch, something like a cat rubbing against your ankle, Joel thought.

"I'm going to take out all mine and lay them on the edge. When we start down, if they want to come they can. If not, they can stay here. They've saved our lives a couple of times already, and I'm not about to risk theirs on this venture." He put the fursnake on the stone and felt about for the rest.

By the time he and Cleery had cleared their clothing of the creatures, they had nine, curling together in some fursnake family reunion on the chilly rock. The sun began to rise behind the farther horizon, and when the light was good enough, Joel hitched a rope harness about his shoulders and started down the cliff. Before he was out of reach, two of the fursnakes slithered down the rope and crawled into his pockets again. He found himself relieved. With two to warn them of the approach of Knackers, they would be in better shape than he had expected.

He resolutely refused to look down past his seeking toes. This Rift was old, it became evident from the weathering of the granite. That was good, because it meant buckling and heaving and other natural upheavals had cracked the stone, weathered out grooves, and given a very poor, almost sheer, but remotely possible route down to the water.

He slipped on his third step downward. The thin rope cut into his back and shoulder, but the two above anchored him until he could find another hold. This was not going to be easy, and if they got down without losing one (maybe all) of his group he was going to be mightily surprised.

He got to the end of his length of rope, found a belaying point, and called up to Helen, "Now you can start down. I've tried to make enough marks to show you where to set your fingers. You sure you can do this?"

Her voice came down clearly. "Motivation is the key. Compared to staying in the Knackers' cannery, this is no trouble at all. I'll bet I could walk across a ceiling, holding on with my fingernails."

Even in his precarious position, Joel grinned. She was right. It was the only thing that had allowed him and Cleery to survive so far.

CHAPTER ELEVEN

He felt the rope jerk and twitch as she made her cautious way toward him. He set his fingers solidly into a good crevice beside the knob of stone and prepared to hold on if she slipped, but she made it within a couple of yards before she lost her footing. He was ready, and Cleery, above them, had a good grip on his end of the rope.

Already Joel was sweating, though the morning was still very cool. The fursnakes had thrust their heads out of his pockets and were watching intently as their alien host held Helen's weight and waited while she found another toehold. When she was set again, Joel went down another few yards, found another solid knob of rock around which to belay the rope, and yelled up to Cleery, "You can start down now, Corp. I have you."

One by one, bit by bit, the three worked their way down the cliff, angling first to one side and then the other to find protrusions capable of bearing the weight of anyone who fell. Slipping and catching, sweating and praying, Joel felt his knees aching with stress. His fingers, already bruised and cut and mangled, tried to go numb, but he kept them alive by pure will power.

When they came to the end of the relatively easier part of the descent, they were still some four or five hundred feet above the water. Below that, the rock was slick and smooth, hardly an unevenness marring its face. Joel located a ledge (earlier in his life he wouldn't have considered that narrow strip of stone to be even a wrinkle in the cliff wall), and the other two settled onto it beside him while they considered how to proceed.

"We have a lot of rope, don't we, if we untie ourselves? More than enough to reach the water?" Helen asked. "Why don't we find someplace to tie off an end and then slide down it, one by one, to the river? Then we could cut off what we couldn't reach and keep the rest in case we need it again."

Joel looked across her tangled mop of hair at Cleery, who grinned. "We're going to have to recruit you, girl, before we're done," the Corp said.

Joel was already edging farther along, searching for some protrusion solid enough to hold their weights in succession, as they went down. Forty yards to his left he found a place where a runnel from above had worn away layers of softer rock from the main body of granite, leaving a needle-like spur as thick as his leg and some meter and a half long.

He caught it with his right hand and shook it hard. It didn't budge. He moved farther aside and pushed at it vigorously. It was part of the cliff, as solid as the unweathered stone on either side. With a sigh of relief, he made a double loop of the rope and tied it off with his very best set of knots.

"Found it," he called to the others. "I'm going to move farther along, and you come, Helen. We'll untie you and you can take the first ride. Then Cleery can follow you, and I'll come last. I want to push the rope away from the ledge with my toe to keep it from fraying."

Helen crept toward him, her fingers white against the ridges she gripped, her feet moving with incredible care along the two-inch ledge. When she reached him, Joel pulled the now-freed rope toward him, measured out his best guess at the distance to the water, and tied a solid loop at that point.

"Catch the rope with both hands. Wrap a turn around your right wrist—that way—and hold it under your arm. Now, when you step off the cliff, keep pushing yourself away with both feet, letting yourself down slowly enough not to burn your hands. When you get to the loop, catch onto it and look down. If it isn't too far, just drop into the water. Even if it is fairly shallow, it will break your fall, and if it is deep you'll go under and bob right up again. All right?"

Her eyes were wide in her pale face, but she nodded. "I saw people rappel down cliffs on holovee. That way?"

"It isn't as easy as it looks, but given our motivation I think we'll all do just fine. Now go." He watched her step off backward, give a gasp, and drop out of sight. Her feet thudded against rock, there was silence, and then they thudded again. "Good girl!" he called.

There was no way to lean out and watch her, and he listened with painful intensity until he heard a distant splash. When he tweaked the rope, it came up easily. She was down, for better or for worse.

Cleery edged toward him, trying to grin but not succeeding very well. "I got a couple of fursnakes too," he said as he caught the rope and prepared to step off. "You know, Karsh, they might be real good help to the military, if we could get a few back to headquarters. But I don't want the officers to think they're nothing but animals and abuse 'em."

Joel guided him off the ledge, keeping the rope clear with his boot toe. "I agree, Corp. We'll think of something. You just get down there safely and see how Helen is doing."

Then he, too, was gone, and only the regular thud of his feet against the cliff told Joel he was going down correctly. There came another splash at last, and the rope hung free in his hands. He tested the spire of rock for one last time and gripped the strand.

It wasn't easy—he'd been right in that department, he learned quickly. The rope was thinner than any he had ever used for rappelling, and the pain in his hands was considerable before he reached the loop. When he looked down he was still quite a distance above the water, but he could see two heads bobbing beside a rock in midstream. Two hands came up and waved him down.

He loosed the loop and dropped, still holding the rope between sleeve and chest. He hit cleanly, going deep. The water was cold and swift. Only the handy rock had kept his companions from being swept downstream. He cut desperately at the rope, as soon as he bobbed to the surface.

He swam toward his companions, and once in the lee of the boulder he found that he could tread water in the comparative calm there. Cleery reached out and bumped his shoulder with a wet fist. "Worked, Karsh. Worked damn good. Now what do we do?"

Joel looked at Helen, who was goose-pimply, her face almost blue. "You all right?"

"F-f-freezing to death," she said between chattering teeth.

"Then we'd better get onto dry land and build a fire." He looked across the stream to the gradual slope of the eastern shore. It was studded with rocks of all sizes, which promised footholds if they could cross to it.

"I'll go," said Cleery. "I swim pretty good." He caught one end of the rope from Joel's hand and set off at once, angling downstream with the force of the current but steadied by Joel's grip on the other end of the line. When he reached the other side he waded out, sat suddenly, and waved.

"You next," Joel said to Helen. "Here, hold onto the line between the two of us. It'll help you keep from being taken off downstream."

When his turn came, he was cold, stiff, and aching in every joint and muscle. The solid ground felt wonderful, but they had no time to enjoy it. They had taken much of the day in their descent. Now the shadow of the cliff darkened the eastern shore; soon night would fall again. Third moon was just rising over the plain beyond the river.

"We've got to find fuel. Those bushes beyond the waterline should do; then we can find someplace sheltered from the wind. There are certainly enough boulders farther along to make me believe it."

Cleery shook himself like a dog, his Combats doing their usual excellent job of shedding water and holding in warmth. Helen, on the other hand, was still draped in his blanket and her scraps of Knacker clothing.

"We'll go get wood," he told her. "You take off everything and shake that blanket hard. It's made to repel water, so it should shake dry. Then wrap yourself up until we can get a fire going. If you feel like it, you might investigate that pile of rocks upstream." He handed her his fursnakes and Cleery contributed his. "Let these wrap around you. They'll help warm you up."

Before he had gone six paces he heard the unmistakable sound of a blanket being shaken, and he nodded. Once they were warm, they could eat some of the concentrates from his and Cleery's packs. Then they'd move again, away from their fire. There was no need to give the Knackers any advantage they didn't already have.

CHAPTER TWELVE

Before third moon was overhead, the three were dry, fed, and located a mile or more downstream from their point of descent. The scrubby bushes on the eastern shore promised quick cover, if Knackers should fly overhead or come along the river. By the time Helen was unable to travel any longer, both Karsh and Cleery were wearier than they liked to admit, and the group sank into a sort of grotto composed of water-carved stone on three sides and bushes on the fourth.

There, with third moon in optimum position for communication, Cleary unpacked the Com unit and keyed in the erratic bursts of Morse that gave their position, told of the release of the prisoner in order to try to capture them, and put into careful terms the presence of the fursnakes.

Joel thought for a while before giving Cleery the words:

> FOUND FRIENDLY NATIVE SPECIES HOSTILE TO KNACKERS. EXHIBIT ABILITY TO WARN APPROACH OF ENEMY FROM SIGNIFICANT DISTANCE.

Once the transmission was completed, they settled together into a huddle, with fursnakes twined around necks and shoulders. In the night a swishing sound roused Karsh, who opened his eyes and saw, against the mist of stars, the dark shape of a Knacker shuttle moving from west to east at an angle to the river.

He clamped his jaw and waited. If they were scanning for life-signs, they would surely pick up his little group. Unless—he stroked the furry creature around his neck—unless the fursnake life-sign confused the reading enough to mislead the seekers. It had, he thought, done that before. Evidently it did it again, for he drifted off to sleep without any further disturbance.

It was a long time before the Com unit burbled its quiet twitter and woke him. Headquarters must have had more information than they could analyze, he thought as he shook Cleery.

When they decoded the message, it gave Joel sudden hope.

CONTINUE ALONG STREAM. PICKUP POINT ONE KLICK PAST FOUR-POINT PEAK. CONTACT WHEN ON SITE. BRING NATIVE SPECIES. WELL DONE.

The last two words shook Joel. Headquarters simply did not pass out compliments, no matter what the troops on the ground might accomplish. What did they want from him? he wondered.

Cleery was thinking along the same lines. "I don't trust those knotheads," he said as he packed away the unit. "They want to do something nasty with the fursnakes, I'd bet on it. We got to do something to save 'em, Karsh. They're good little fellows and don't deserve what HQ might do."

CHAPTER THIRTEEN

As they repacked their supplies and headed out into the dimness of pre-dawn, Joel was thinking about that, as well as other, more immediate matters. The farther they moved along the stream, the stranger the scent of the air became. At first fresh and clean, the odor became acrid, with a hint of mold or rot or something even less pleasing.

The sun rose slowly as they traveled, and they edged away from the water into the scrub, keeping as close to cover as possible. When the fursnakes began to hiss, Joel started to run into the overgrown flats beside them, but the little creatures convulsed with protest. Taking the hint, Joel moved back into the rocks, but the fursnakes kept looking upstream and inland, as if some concentration of Knackers might lurk there.

At last he ordered Cleery and Helen into hiding among a tangle of waterweed and willow-like growth. There was a spike of stone just beyond that spot, and he wrapped a fursnake around his neck and began shin-nying up its weathered column. The animal seemed not to object, but when he reached the top he under-stood why it had been so upset.

Over a large stretch of scrub bushes, several acres in extent, stretched a thick webbing, binding the scrub together into a lumpy carpet. Occasional huge lumps of pearly stuff were visible through the web, and near every one of them was a bulk that was disturbing in its resemblance to a human figure.

Clinging to the column, though sheltering his body behind it and peering around one side, Joel watched the web closely. Motion at the farther edge alerted him, and he shivered as a Knacker, this one more bulgy than the warrior Knackers, picked its many-legged way into the complex, seemed to choose a spot, and began laying eggs. This was a damn Knacker hatchery! Even as he stared, the female completed her laying and began spinning layers of webbing over the eggs. Then she retreated beyond the web, only to return with a stiff human body that she sealed into her offspring's silky cradle.

She seemed completely unaware of his presence as she completed her task and retreated cautiously beyond the limits of the webbing. Once she was gone, Joel descended the column and knelt beside his companions, who listened, wide-eyed, as he described his discovery.

"Surely we can manage to destroy this batch," he concluded. "But I don't see how. I have a feeling any twitch on that web is going to bring a bunch of Mamas scurrying to defend their young."

Cleery was looking thoughtful. "What about the fursnakes? They seem to hate the critters a lot. Why not aim one or two at the web and see what they do?"

Joel nodded. "Might work, and if it doesn't we're no worse off. I thought of setting fire to the web, but those men are in there—they might still be alive, just enough to know they were burning to death. I've read about spiders on other worlds that sort of paralyze their victims and leave them alive to feed the young."

Cleery volunteered to creep close enough to let the fursnakes make up their minds. Joel, however, was unable to remain behind, and Helen refused to stay alone. So they were all together, hidden by both rocks and shrubbery, when the fursnakes sensed the hatchery and bristled along their entire furry lengths.

One headed toward the middle of the field, one to the left, one to the right. In a moment they were gone, without disturbing a strand of the webbing that lay much higher in the bushes than the level along which they could travel.

No sign of struggle, no hint of motion flexed the web. Joel began worrying that the creatures had been trapped, somehow, in the Knacker hatchery. There was nothing to do but wait, and together the three hid, while the sun moved overhead and began descending toward the looming lip of the cliff.

Before its shadow quite reached their hiding place, the first fursnake returned, limp and exhausted. Joel took it up and discovered that much of its length must be a poison gland ending in its fangs, for the animal was thinner by a third than it had been earlier. Joel noticed a fluid about to drip from a fang, and he caught it on a leaf. From that he transferred it into a vial from his pack. Having a sample of the fursnake poison might well help him persuade his superiors that it would be impossible to force the creatures to obey human commands.

Obviously the animal and its fellows had spent these long hours biting Knacker young, still encased in their eggs. When the others returned, they, too, were thinner and very weary. All of the creatures slithered away into the rocks, where they evidently found some source of nourishment. They returned at dark, sleek and renewed.

CHAPTER FOURTEEN

With most of a day of rest to sustain them, the group moved forward in darkness, helped along by the glimmer of the vast star field above and the reflection of stars in the water beside them. It was best to be far away before the Knacker nursery-keepers found that their charges—at least some of them—were dead.

They traveled desperately for two days, keeping always near the cover of bushes or boulders. At last they faced a long stretch of river running almost straight toward the peak that was their goal. The eastern shore was now rising, trapping them between its increasing high wall and the water. There was no concealment other than the stream itself, which ran fast and deep between ridges of stone.

"We'd better run like hell, once it's dark," Cleary said. "I don't like the looks of this one little bit. If anything flies over, or if the Knackers keep watch from that peak up there, we're in deep trouble."

Helen nodded, and Joel grunted. "You're dead right, Corp. If we're to get past that peak, we've got to make time like never before. And here we are worn to the bone, getting hungry, boots wearing out—those that have them," he amended, looking down at Helen's feet, which she had wrapped in strips cut from the all-purpose blanket.

Again the sun was behind the far edge of the Rift, though the sky was still filled with sunlight and distant, circling birds. "As soon as the shadow is deep enough, we'd better start. We'll rest now, and eat whatever is left, because we're not going to have any time to stop until we get beyond that peak." The shadow seemed to creep across the river, edging toward them with terrible slowness. They had slept for a while, eaten what they could, but Joel was too near his goal to relax for long, and the others had the same problem. Long before it was dark enough, they had the packs ready, Helen's feet wrapped in fresh folds of blanket, and the fursnakes coiled in pockets and inside shirts.

Twice distant shadows across the sky marked the passing of Knacker shuttles. There was no way to know what had really occurred back in the nursery field, or how the caregivers reacted. Did Knackers have any feeling for their young? Joel pushed away the thought.

When they moved out at last, it was one at a time, Cleery going first, finding a deep shadow in which to crouch, and waiting for Helen to join him. When she arrived, Cleery went forward, then Helen, and Joel came behind, keeping a watchful eye on the rear. He had a feeling that something was behind, following, but there was never any sound or sign of a pursuer.

They moved surprisingly fast, for once it was fully dark they didn't hide but went on, single file, skirting the water's edge, avoiding the water-rounded stones. The peak, dark against the spangle of stars, disappeared behind the adjacent cliff, and only when they at last came to a double-bend in the watercourse could they see its sharp points again.

Joel measured their distances with anxious accuracy, trying to pinpoint the spot mentioned as the pickup point. He wasted his time, for when they reached it he knew it at once. On the side of the river that was now northeast, a flat bowl, hollowed by some past whirlpool and then raised by the movements of the strata beneath, promised easy access for a shuttle.

It was almost concealed, even from the top of the mountain beyond the cliff. Once they were within its deep curve, the three felt themselves hidden from observation.

Joel gestured to Cleery, who unpacked the Com unit and sent news of their arrival crackling into space. Then they huddled under the riverward lip of the bowl and waited again.

CHAPTER FIFTEEN

The fursnakes began hissing furiously. Joel readied his weapon, hearing Cleery do the same, while Helen moved back against the rocky wall. The scritch-scratch of Knacker feet came to Joel's ears, as one of the spider-creatures stalked into the other side of the cup and sank amid its knees, as if to wait. The fursnakes slid away, invisible in the dimness, but Joel felt sure they were moving toward the Knacker. He watched closely, but until the enemy kindled some kind of blue-white flare he could not see them at all. Even then, they were only ripples of unobtrusive motion, until they reached the Knacker's hairy feet.

Then they were visible indeed. They swarmed up the many-jointed legs, converging on the man-shaped body. The Knacker convulsed, struggled, quivered, danced...and settled slowly to one side like a sinking ship. Dead, it seemed to sink in upon itself, a heap of dust-colored wisps instead of the huge consumer of human flesh.

The fursnakes reappeared silently, but Joel knew he must send them away. The dead Knacker would be all the reason he needed for keeping the possessors of such virulent poison away from the forces of humankind.

He wondered if analysis of his sample and of that corpse's biochemistry might supply humanity with one weapon useful against this enemy. That would be enough for the fursnakes to contribute.

He took up the lithe creatures, one by one, stroked them, then flipped them over the lip of the cup. As the last one disappeared, the pickup shuttle settled quietly into the depression, and Cleery and Helen ran toward it.

"In! In! Hurry!" snapped the voice of the sergeant in charge. "Troopers—two. Check. Female human, former prisoner. Check. Alien creatures? Where are they?" he grated.

Joel paused at the ramp. "Look over there. You'll want to take that Knacker back to the labs. The alien beings just killed it a couple of minutes ago. They took off, and we didn't feel we could stop anything that can kill a Knacker with one bite."

The Sergeant stared at him for an instant. Then he sent two men to gather up the remains in a body-bag, though it took quite a lot of folding and bending to make it fit.

"Tough customers, eh?" he asked, as the shuttle sighed into the air and headed for the third moon.

"Very," said Joel. "Helpful but dangerous, if you get my drift."

The sergeant looked grim. "HQ wanted to see those critters. They won't be happy about this."

Cleery leaned forward, his eyes gleaming in the

light from the telltales. "They better check out that poison first. We got another sample, too, right here." He grinned at Joel and Helen, who sat together opposite him. "Not the sort you can bully, those little guys," he said.

The sergeant squinted at them, his experienced gaze taking in much that was unsaid. "Like that, eh?" he asked.

"Like that," said Joel Karsh, before settling back as comfortably as possible and considering the possibility that he might live for a few months more.

Now he and Cleery knew things about the Knackers and their local enemies that would be valuable. They had traveled the Rift, which the Knackers seemed to consider impassable terrain. And Headquarters had a poison that killed Knackers and a body to analyze to learn its vulnerable points.

It might be that their failed sortie had resulted in enough new information to begin tipping the balance in this unsought and miserable war. He hoped so. Then he dropped off to sleep, completely relaxed for the first time in days. Maybe he would live to buy that farm, after all.

ABOUT THE AUTHOR

The author of seventy books, more than forty of them published commercially, ARDATH MAYHAR began her career in the early eighties with science fiction novels from Doubleday and TSR, and Atheneum. Changing focus, she wrote westerns (as **Frank Cannon**) and mountain man novels (as **John Killdeer**), four prehistoric Indian books under her own name, and historical western *High Mountain Winter* under the byline **Frances Hurst**. Many of her novels and collections are being reprinted or published by the Borgo Press Imprint of Wildside Press.

Now eighty, Mayhar was widowed in 1999, after forty-one years of marriage, and has four grown sons. She works at home, writing short fiction and nonfiction, and doing book doctoring professionally. Her web pages can be found at:

w2.netdot.com/ardathm/

and

http://ofearna.us/books/mayhar.html

KNACK' ATTACK

On the bucolic farming planet of Terr'ferme, Rabbs din Chorest, the fifteen-year-old youngest child of the Chorest-Grant, has just been made Hand, being sent to the Blackmarker Hills to tend a herd of clorses (cloned horses) and beefers. Not far away is the ruin of Spire-town, a long-abandoned place of the Old-uns, a race that had once inhabited this world.

Then the Knack's invade, destroying settlements, devastating ranches, and harvesting human and large animal flesh for reprocessing as food. Rabbs is cut off from civilization, with no way of communicating with the outside world. When a party of refugees appears, they become the Hand's responsibility as well. Trapped by a bug troop in a cave near the ruined alien city, the humans have nowhere to go and no one to ask for help.

Will anyone survive the Knack' attack?

Selected Borgo Press Books by ROBERT REGINALD

Academentia: A Future Dystopia
Ancestral Voices: An Anthology of Early Science Fiction (ed.)
Ancient Hauntings (ed. with Douglas Menville)
The Attempted Assassination of John F. Kennedy
BP 300: A Bibliography of The Borgo Press, 1976-1998
Choice Words: The Borgo Press Book of Writers Writing About Writing (ed.)
Classics of Fantastic Literature (with Douglas Menville)
Contemporary Science Fiction Authors
The Coyote Chronicles: A Chronological History of California State University, San Bernardino, 1960-2010
Cumulative Paperback Index, 1939-1959
Dreamers of Dreams (ed. with Douglas Menville)
The Elder of Days: Tales of the Elders
Forgotten Fantasy, Issues #1-5 (ed. with Douglas Menville)
Guide to SF & Fantasy in Library of Congress Classification
The House of the Burgesses (with Mary Burgess)
If J.F.K. Had Lived: A Political Scenario (with Jeffrey Elliot)
The Judgment of the Gods and Other Verdicts of History
King Solomon's Children (ed. with Douglas Menville)
Knack' Attack: A Tale of the Human-Knacker War
Mystery & Detective Fiction in Library of Congress Class.
The Nasty Gnomes: A Novel of the Phantom Detective
Our Favorite Eats in the Inland Empire (with John Weeks)
The Paperback Show Murders
Phantasmagoria (ed. with Douglas Menville)
The Phantom's Phantom: A Novel of the Phantom Detective
R.I.P. (ed. with Douglas Menville)
Science Fiction & Fantasy Book Review (ed. with N. Barron)
Science Fiction & Fantasy Literature
They (ed. with Douglas Menville)
Worlds of Never (ed. with Douglas Menville)
Xenografitti: Essays on Fantastic Literature

KNACK' ATTACK

A TALE OF THE HUMAN-KNACKER WAR

ROBERT REGINALD

THE BORGO PRESS
MMX

KNACK' ATTACK

DEDICATION

For

Anna and Sarah and Makayla and Kylee—

The Future

CONTENTS

PROLOGUE
"They're Your 'Sponsibility Now"

I jus' keeps thinkin' about the last thin' my Dads e'er told me.

"Rabbs," he said, "They're your 'sponsibility now."

He was talkin' 'bout the clorses and beefers in the south pasture. They'd been growed from Old Earth stock umpteen generations ago, and 'dapted to our world nigh 'fore it was settled, more 'n' 500 years 'go. I don't ken that science stuff much, but without some changes deep down 'side, none of our stock could've et anythin' here. Somethin' 'bout bad "bilogie," Teach Bets had said. Prob'ly true of us-un-folks as well.

Yeah, yeah, I knows I's s'posed to talk 'bout what happed on Terr'ferme, why I lived and all, why I sur*vivaled*. Wellaway, I don't *knows* why it is I lived, Meester—the Lord God 'bove be my troth!—and I don't *knows* why Dads, he had to die, and I don't *knows* why I had to leave ev'ry-un and ev'rythin' that I knew and loved and come 'way out here to this cold bare rock.

And I don't really wants to think about it now

neither, tell me no lies. But those words of his, I keeps on hearin' them rollin' 'round 'side me: *"They're your 'sponsibility now."*

It was *how* he said it, see, 'most like a command, like I was real growner or somethin'—and I'd best do a damgood job too, and or I'd be hearin' 'bout it some-times soontimes.

I saved what I could, Dads, I saved what I could. I really did, truth be told.

So this is how it came to be, Meester, best's I can recall. This is what happed when the Knack's, they came down 'pon poor Terr'ferme-Land.

PART ONE
THE COMIN' OF THE KNACK'S

CHAPTER ONE
"Time to Git Yourself Goin'"

That day, it started jus' like any other, though 'twas somethin' real-special-like to me. Dads shook me 'wake at 2820, 'bout an hour 'fore the suns came up, sayin', "Come on, now, Rabbitface, time to git yourself goin' 'gain." He'd been callin' me that of late, jus' like he did when I was a young-un. (But that's *not* my name, Meester, not really.)

I ain't no early-birdy, nosiree, but I fell out of my 'droll, splashed some cold awa on my face, gave thanks to the fertsump, and threw on three shirts, two pantaloons, and a pair of comfy old work boots.

By this time Dads had thrown some grub t'gether for us-uns and the hands—but the only ones left at Stead right then were old Adryans and Tamzyn, the rest bein' out and 'bout and such.

We chowed on some hot mealyworms and pseudwheat and frittered saussiss, all washed down with raw clorse milk, and after I belched my 'preciation twice or thrice, which was the only polite thin' to do, I helped with the cleanin'-up, dryin' whilst Tamzyn washed, in the old-fashioned way we did. Yeah, yeah, gadgets we

had every-which-way, but somethin's were still better done with joy-and-love.

Aftertimes, I puts on my 'veralls and screenhat and bugmist and 'qualizer, and then saddled up Meez Lambo, my rouge range beefer. Dads gave me a quick hands-up, handed me my stick, and I was as ready as any Hand could be—and damproud of the fact, yessiree.

I sat up straight-and-stiff, knowin' that this was *my* day, my time to shine in the twin suns. Dads looked at me strange-like then, like he saw what was comin', and he smiled, jus' for a moment, stroked the point of his grayish beard with his left hand, and said: "Rabbs, they're your 'sponsibility now. You take care out there, you hear?"

But I was eager-beaver to head on out, so I jus' tipped my stick in the Hand's olden salute, dropped the visor o'er my face, chk-chked to Meez Lambo, and turned my beefer t'wards the red slice of Griswold easin' up o'er the 'rizon. My steed grunted out loud, hunkered down in that let's-git-down-to-it slopey stance they have, and moved forward on the road. We headed out the auto-gate, which closed right tight behind us, givin' us-uns a final snick-snack of goodluck-goodbye-love. If only I'd known how "goodbye" that sound, it really was.

We kept to Muskoy Trail for a coupla klicks, and then ranged southwest t'wards the Blackmarkers, the best grazin' lands on all Chorest-Spread. 'Course, I'd been out this way many times 'fore, but never like this, never runnin' my ownsome self.

That was the why of it, you see.

Billieboy'd been called to Service to fight the Knack's, ninemonth past, and J. C.'d been drafted to Versity-Force three months since, and Moms, well, we didn't know where she was, and Dads, he jus' wouldn't say. She'd been gone a year or more by then, and we didn't talk 'bout it at table, or anywheres else neither. The one time I'd tried to dig the thin' out of its place, Dads'd lost his goodwill, and after that, none of us-uns had had the gumption to respeak the thin'. It jus' sorta sat there gittin' cold and lumpy on the bench, if you knows what I mean.

I dreams 'bout her sometimes. She was real smart-like, see, and I picture her doin' the guvment work somewheres, or helpin' with the war 'gainst the Knack's, and bein' told to keep the peace from all young-uns. But I knows in the heart that goes pitty-patty deep within my chest that she run off with some-un, and I ain't never goin' to see her perty face 'gain. Pardon me my tearies, Meester: it's a hard life we do lead, to be sure.

So the far way and the near way was this: that my Dads, he came to me one day, and he said: "Rabbs, I needs you to do this somethin' for me"—and I knew my growed time had come at last. And I was ready, yessiree, to take up my stick and do the deeds that had to be done.

And now I was an hourride from our Stead, slowly movin' into the Blackmarkers, whilst Griswold's little yellow sister, Gorgonio, shyly peeped out from

between the hills as she woke from her daily rest. Crowdin' 'round me as I climbed the wand'rin' trail were Fredons, Crastos, Biltz, Makrost, and the other dark spires that gave this range its name.

Teach'd once said that some geo-'nominon had made the black-tops to bust out of their ground; but in my dreams, I saw the Old-uns, the ones who lived 'fore man came down to this place, and they were the folks who gathered in circles and said, "So it be!"— and 'twas done. Then they took their rest, and their dwellin's stay silent now, silent with the noise of their hidden passage, and no-un goes there much. But I've been there, oh yes I have, many a time.

What's that? Sorry, Meester, for roamin' so far from the true path.

Now, as I said, I was comin' up into the Blackmarkers, that's where I was, and Meez Lambo, she stopped sudden-like and put her head in the air, snortin' a coupla times, whuff-whuffin' the way the beefers do, and then she tugged the reins to the left. I gave her her teeth, 'cause she knew what I needed then, and I let her go as she would.

Sev'ral times she stopped and snuffed, and each time she changed her way a bit, jus' slightly, and by the time that Gorgonio was kissin' ole Griswold on high, we were gittin' nigh unto our goal, I could tell. We came to a crik called Baldy-Run, which danced out of the hills with a white-frothy joy, cold and clear and full of cheer; and there we found Seer Maks, Dads' old-Hand, whose place I was to take.

"Rabbs," he said, from where he was stooped down next to the fire, "now what brin's you out into these-here parts?"

"Seer Hand," I said, "Dads said that I takes your place, and right quick now."

"He said that, did he? Wellaway, you've come into your ownsome at last, then. Joy and good harvest, Rabbs din Chorest! I gather you to the community of Hands."

He helped me down from the beefer, which I tied to a nearby tree; and then offered me, he did, an empty metal cup, and poured into it a finn of liquid from a flask. He did the same for hisself, and t'gether we sipped one small drink from the water of life, the awa vita, as some have said. Then we tossed the rest of the brew onto the flames of the fire, which flared high its response.

"Joy and good harvest, Seer Maks," I said.

"Well spoken, Hand Rabbs," he said. Then he began packin' his gear, and stowin' it tight-and-right for his travel-time.

"The clorses, they roam nigh unto the Spiretown of the Old-uns," he said whilst wand'rin' through the site, pickin' up this and that, "'bout four or five klicks o'er there"—he pointed due southways—"and the beefers are sidewise to them two klicks nigh westerly. Plenteous feed and water in them parts. Nighttimes, I keeps 'em in Kopps-Vale, yonderish."

Soon he was ready to head back to Stead, and he whistled twice for his beefer, Seer Mabouls, who came

trottin' up the crik so quick-like that he nigh bowled o'er his Meester.

"Whoa, now," Seer Maks said, holdin' out somethin' in his right hand. The beastie poked out his lon' tongue and gobbed up the sweet, and then would have done anythin' that he wanted him to do, jus' for another go.

But Seer Maks, he planted his left foot in the stirrup and swung hisself up on the saddle, noddin' his stick at my made Handship, and followed the suns back t'wards the Stead.

I looked o'er the empty site, but decided to move my ownsome camp nigher unto my cares, and after mountin' my range beefer once 'gain, I followed the Baldy-Run-Crik upstream t'wards the Spiretown of the Old-uns.

CHAPTER TWO
"By What Sign Do You Pass?"

The crik, it runs through the Spiretown, though hidden-like for some ways, as I knew from my early wandries there; but no-un likes bein' in that place once the suns, they take their ownsome rest.

I sees the doubt shinin' in your eyes, Meester, but you don't know these thin's save from bookish reads. I been there, you ain't, and that's a truth to be told.

So I made my place in the Mentons-Vale, half a klick 'fore the Town, where the Baldy-Run does shallow. The hills there spread their win's to either side, and the trees grow thick, and the grazin's real damgood.

'Twas a well-known route-place on Chorest-Grant, so I needs do nothin' more than to clean out the flamepit and add some more drysticks to the pyre-pile. Then I remounted Meez Lambo, and went out to seek out my chores, knowin' that I needed to herd them back to the Vale for the dusky-time.

Why did I do this, you ask? 'Cause beefers and clorses, though they may wander the 'Markers at will under the watchful eyes of the sunny-twins, must shelter themselves when Griswold and Gorgonio go

off to their ownsome beds. The chasers, they creep out from their holes with the comin' of the dark, and must be kept to their usual prey. That was the Hand's job, see: that was why I was here.

I found the twelve clorses nigh unto where Seer Maks had said, up on the Bildenbeks, and with Meez Lambo's help, moved them to where I thought the six beefers to be. Then we led them on a merry-way down the Brisko-Crik-Vale to where it kissed and merged with the Baldy-Run.

'Round the next bend was the Spiretown, and I spied a campment nigh thereto, with growed folks who were comin' and goin' from tent to town. I left Meez Lambo to hold the flocks tight, and skedaddled o'er to that place, 'cause no-un had told me of this ruckus happin' on our lands.

A tall-woman stepped from the huts to block my way. "Wisdom and joy in all your days," she said. "I's Mays din Kotts, Doc and Lead of these studiants."

"I be Hand Rabbs din Chorest," I said, standin' ownself straight and holdin' high my stick. In this thin' I was Stead for my Dads. "And this be the Chorest-Grant. By what sign do you pass?"

She unfolded her left hand, holdin' wide the five finners, where I could scan them with my staff. The counter and sign were there, sure 'nough, so she had the right of it.

"Joy and wisdom to you and yours," I said. "What study do you make here?"

"We follow the ways of the Old-uns," she said. "We

wish to learn how they lived, and how they died."

"'Tis not a place, the Spiretown, where one may dig the ground-holes."

"This be true," she said, "but other probin's can be made. Do you wish to look-see…?"

I sighed, for truth to tell, I would've spent a ten-day or more in Spiretown, could I have learned somethin' new of the Old-uns—but I had other 'sponsibilities now.

"Night will come to us-uns soonest," I said, "and I must go to put to bed my beasties. But I thank you most kindly for the 'vitation. T'morrow, p'raps?"

"T'morrow, to be sure," she said. "Where be you?"

"In Mentons-Vale," I said, "not 'lon' down the crik from here."

And then I went back to my herd, mounted Meez Lambo once more, and found the camp-place half a klick onward. I used my stick to set the bounds, from standin' stone to standin' stone, 'round and 'bout-like, and then lit the pyre, warmin' some grub from my pack. By the time I settled back 'gainst the grass, belly-full and beasties quiet, Gorgonio was startin' to set 'neath the rim of the hill.

'Tis a strange thin' that Teach could never 'splain to me, that somedays Gorgonio finds her rest first, and somedays 'tis her sister, Meez Griswold. Meez Bets once put a 'quation 'fore my eyes, sayin' this would tell me so, but such thin's jus' make my brain hurt all o'er—and I didn't ken her learnin'.

Jus' thinkin' about the suns made me yawn my

mouth out wide, so I shook the sleep roughly from my shoulders, and walked the walk of the righteous Hand, checkin' my beasties, and probin' my line. Then I linked my stick to the grid that I'd made, sat back down on my site, and 'lowed my eyes to settle down 'neath their lashes.

But 'tweren't the chasers that brought me right up from the ole sleepytime, nosiree. The sky, it went boom-boom-boom, and the ground, it shook with its grumblin', and everywhichways I saw lightnin's of green and red and yellow. I watched and I watched until my neck started to ache. Whate'er could this be up there?

Then the beasties began lowin' and moanin' in pain and in fear, and I had to tend to them fast, 'cause my line wouldn't hold if they all 'cided to run at once-like. I went to the beefers first, the big-uns, and calmed them down with soothin' talk and 'lectro-shock from my stick, touchin' each at the back of the head, jus' betwixt the horns, startin' with Meez Lambo, their Lead. When they'd been milded 'gain, I put my arms 'round each of the clorses in turn, and one-by-un they bent their knees and went to ground, bowin' themselves to my 'thority. O'er and o'er that night I made the rounds of my camp, doin' what needs to be done to make my beasties safe.

But how safe would they be from the great grand ruckus playin' out in the sky? Truth to tell, how safe would any of us-uns be?

CHAPTER THREE
"They've Come Down to Terr'ferme"

The Twins took their ownsome time in wakin' from that lon', lon' night, or so it seemed to me, but fin'lly the rim of the world began to pink up, and I knew that Meez Griswold would soon make her rosy-finned dawn. With the comin' of the light, the beasties settled down to their rest, though I could still hear the sometime ringin' of the heavens high o'er my head.

I was weary unto the very toes of my feet, for I'd seen little sleep in that o'erlon' night.

Then I heared a buzzin' up the Vale, and e'en as I kenned the sound, it growed and it growed, till an aerolift peered sudden-like 'round the bend. The car settled on a wide space nigh the crik, and Doc Mays popped open the top.

"The Knackers, they've come down to Terr'ferme," she shouted at me from the open cab. "Hand Rabbs, you must decamp. Come back with us to Pompez-Town. You'll be safe-not-sorry there."

I'd heared tell of the Knack's, how they came from the sky and killed all that they found, on world after

world. Bro' Bills had gone to stomp out the bugs ninemonth since, but no word had we heared from him since-time, only tales that growed and growed with the tellin', from them that knew nothin' at all 'bout the real thin's goin' on out there.

The reddish light of Meez Griswold lent fins of fire to the hills of the Blackmarkers, and fire too to the fur of my ownsome childrens, and I knew what my answer must be.

"Sorry, Doc Mays," I said, "but these beasties, they're my 'sponsibility now. If the Knack's, they come to this place, I fight for my right—and for theirs."

She bowed her head without sayin' more words, for what words could she say more than that?—and she then pulled the top of her lift back down, flew her car back to the Spiretown camp, and left that place for good with her folks soontime later. I did not see her 'gain in all the days to come.

Now, Meester, you think me a damfool, I can see, for choosin' to stay in that place with no way to fight those that might come down 'gainst us, but a child of Chorest-Grant is born with more sense than most menkind, as you shall see. I was the last of my five to be borned, but I gained the wits of all those who come before me.

And I, I no damfool, nosiree!

I broke the 'lectro-chain that I'd made 'round my camp, watered the flames in the pit with my juice, and mounted Meez Lambo, chawin' on some drymeat to help break my fast. No time there was for fancies and

such, no time 't'all for rest nor relax. I knew what I needed to do.

Then I led my flock up the crik, makin' them move more fast-like than their usual wont, for I 'membered what I'd seen once-upon-a-time o'er nigh to the Spiretown, when I was yet elevenish in the years, or p'raps twelvish.

No matter that the growners had said to us young-uns, "Go not there!" We went where we would, all of us, and I, the youngest, was wild to see our world in the great Chorest-Grant.

So, on that fine day, I found my way to the place of the Old-uns, and reason played no part 't'all in my pathin'. I wandered hither and thither throughout the Blackmarkers, and when the storm fin'lly splashed upon me—and a surprise for sure it was—I sought shelter in the spires of that lon'-emptied place.

Now, when a man builds hisself a home, he says unto his other, "This is what I sees 'side when I thinks of a place to live," and the other says yea or nay, as she or he feels, and so 'tis made as they will and decide t'gether. But each house has its walls, and each house has its rooms, and each house has many of the same thin's from place to place, for a man wants his nighers to think well of him and his.

But the Spiretown of the Old-uns was not like that. Each place within was diff'rent from t'others. Some had walls, some did not. Some had rooms, some did not. Some had chairs made from stone, some did not. Each was diff'rent too in its ownsome makin', and yet

each had the mark of the Old-uns on it, somethin' that I cannot 'xplain to one who was not there.

Not far from that place was a hillside made of sheer rockface, pocked with holes from some ancient day, and I knew that some of these had flat floors and broad rooms where I could find shelter for the beasties, if needed; and with my stick, I could keep most any 'nemy from out my narrow chamber door. That was what I sought, for no-un would spend a night in the Spiretown, with its strange sounds and whistly winds. I was there once when the suns went down, and I don't think of that time now, never.

When we reached the Spiretown-Vale, I let the beasties run free, and set my camp in front of the largest cave. By then the suns were climbin' up into the sky, and I could still see flashes of light and puffs of smoke there, and hear the growlin' of the heavens, though they were less noisy now than they were before.

Aftertimes, I wandered down to the camp of the studiants, but Doc Mays and her peoples were lon'-gone, as she had promised, though they'd left their huts and 'quipment and such in the dust of their ownsome leavin'.

I heared a noise from one of the tents, and tried enterin' the door, which opened when I turned the latch. They'd left a commset in place, tuned to a station that gave nothin' but static now.

I sat myself down in front of the thin', and turned the dial to another settin'—and another, and another, until suddenly I heared:

"…Mots-Town destroyed, Knackers comin' down the pike there; need help real quick-like. Knack ship hit by Seer Efflans at Courlo-Vale; Seer Efflans movin' to Pastris-Ville to help defensin' there. Callin' Gen'ral Malts, callin' Gen'ral Malts. SpaceForce withdrawin' from the system till more ships arrive. Teebos…."

I shut the damthin' off. The news just hurt my head. I wondered what was happenin' at Chorest-Stead, and where Dads and the Hands had gone. They had no means of defendin' themselves, I knew. I stepped outside to look for distant signs, but the hills, they blocked my view that-ways.

The twins were now chasin' each other high up into the sky, so I still had hours yet to go before their rest. I decided to climb the Khols-Hill, which lay to the west of the Spiretown, 'cause of its easy slope in had. I whistled for Meez Lambo, and when she 'rived, climbed into the saddle once more, and followed a rough trail up and 'round the rise.

When I reached the top, I sat up as high-up as I could on my beefer, pulled out my ranger-viewer, and swept the 'rizon on all sides. Vision to the east was blocked by the great stone hill loomin' 'hind the Spiretown. To the north I could see a largish cloud of smoke oozin' out from where the Pompez-Town should be, and I knew then that Doc Mays and friends would not be comin' back. I felt the hurt deep down 'side, but could not let myself go into the mournin'-time.

In the northwest, where Chorest-Stead stood, I saw nothin' to tell me what had happened there. Southwest

was smudged by 'nother big puff of black smoke, 'bout where the Brelan-Town was sited. Then I heared a far-distant rumble, like unto the herald of a comin' thunderboomer, but could not place the d'rection of the strike.

I don't know how many hours I spent up on that hill, tryin' to ken the what and where and why of the war, and growin' e'er more sad as the time, it passed me by—till I realized that 'twould be darkish soon, and I needed to git my beasties safely boarded up for the night.

And then somethin' odd happed.

The Khols-Hill, jus' like all the highs surroundin' the Spiretown, was topped with a dark spear of sharp rock that pierced the air at the mound's highest point. I heared a cracklin' noise to my right, where the spire was, and snapped my head in that d'rection. I thought I saw a flash of pale green light bein' spit from the top of the thin', jus' for a sec. And then it was gone, and I wondered to myself whether the end of all thin's, or so it seemed to me, was turnin' my brain to clorse-cheese.

"'Tis 'nough," I said out loud, and then kneed my beefer to hop on down that trail before the darkness, it fell 'pon us.

But that night, within the 'lectro-corral of my own makin', I thought again of what I'd visioned that day, and I knew that what I'd seen up on the Khols-Hill was a true thin', not some vap'rous 'maginin' of a untried young-un.

That spire, there was power in it!

CHAPTER FOUR

"Whilst I Lived, the Chorest-Grant Yet Lived"

At the next dawn of morn, as soon as the twins had pulled themselves into the sky, I loosed the beasties to their graze, for they had to feed—and that got me to thinkin' real serious-like 'bout my path here.

When the knack's came—and I knew they would, t'morrow near or t'morrow far—I could 'lectro-block the cave with my stick, but for how lon'? I looked up into the heavens for my answers, but the Lord God, He did not appear at the Spiretown camp to 'lighten me; and I knew jus' then how little I knew of ev'rythin' that I needed to know. It wasn't fair, it wasn't right, but this is what I had.

I looked more closely at my stick, holdin' it up in front of my face. I flicked back the smallish lid on the stem, and saw the greenish light shinin' there. I sighed, 'cause I knew this much: if the satcomlink failed, so would the grid that fed my stick—and then, oh so sad to say, Hand Rabbs, my stick would last no more than a week, if luck shadowed my steps—and much less if not.

And then that light, it would slowly die.

And then my beasties, they too would die.

And then, Meester Spacer, *I* would die.

This was not what I desired—I who'd jus' been made Hand in this, my fifteenth year. And I was a good Hand too, true to the callin' that had been passed unto me.

But whate'er could I do?

I went down to the camp of the studiants, and turned on the commlink once more, but the messages were sadder than they'd been on the yestereve, and harder to find on the dial. This is the way 'twould go, I could see for myself: day by day, fewer and fewer they would be, until soon there'd be no voices 't'all for me to hear. And then all that would be left in this world would be the Hand and the beasties—and sim'lar-like else and where, little bits and bites of humankind, till ev'rythin' and ev'ry-un would become eats for the Knack's.

Think, Rabbs, I said to myself. *Think!*

E'en could I protect myself and my flock in the caves, e'en if I had all the 'lectro-shocks that I needed, how would my beasties et? I had seven beefers in my care—big-uns too, the smallest at least twenty-one hands high—and a dozen of the petite clorses, maybe nine or ten hands high. They all needed fresh clon-grass, piles of it, or wheat-stack, if the green stuff couldn't be found. In those bare holes in the rock, there was nothin' of neither.

And what of the awa? I knew that at least one of the caves had sprun' a sprin' deep within its depths, but the beefers couldn't git themselves down there, no

ways, and I had no means of brin'in' the water up to them, save by slow totes which would not be 'nough to nourish them.

At every junction, I found a blockage on the road, and I didn't know what I could do. There was no safe place to rest my cares, no dear Dads that I could call 'pon for help, e'en if I'd had the means. No one and nothin' out there.

But still I had myself, and that would either be 'nough—or 'twouldn't. No point in cryin' jus' 'cause thin's were startin' to git tough out there.

I decided to see what the studiants had left behind, when they'd scooted so quickly 'way to their doom. For the rest of that day, save for keepin' an ear out for the beasties, and makin' the rounds ev'ry so often, I went from hut to hut in the camp, lookin' at what might be the most useful to me when the Knack's, they fin'lly did come.

I found food and drink locked 'way in airtight cartons, and a crate of sticks, all of them charged, and an aerolift parked in a shed (though I could not seem to power the thin'), and a crawler that worked, and a few weapons (shooters, mostly, not much good for anythin' save plinkin' chasers and the other small critters), and a small machine that I thought was meant to help produce 'lectro-power in case the grid went down— that-un might help a bit.

I told to myself that I had five days, maybe more, to git ready for the Knack's. They wouldn't travel this far out from the towns till they'd finished what they were

doin' there.

When the night stretched its hands o'er the land once more, I retreated with my beasties to the safe-corral I'd made near the Big-Cave on the Rock-Hill, and munched on the munchies that I'd found in the camp.

I wondered then what Dads had done, and whether the Stead still stood, and who had lived and who had died in the land. I didn't feel so good aftertimes, but the thought had to be thought jus' the same. No good runnin' 'way from the bad news.

And I 'cided, in the end, that they were all gone now, and I needed to live my life with that notion in mind. I had my 'sponsibility here, bein' the 'sponsibility of any Hand: to save, preserve, and help those given unto my care. That was my first and only chore, comin' e'en 'fore my ownsome livin'. Yet, whilst I lived, the Chorest-Grant yet lived.

That's still to be true, Meester Spacer, still to be true, e'en on this dead cold rock of yours.

CHAPTER FIVE
"The Grid Was Yet Live"

I was up with Meez Griswold on the mornin' of the fourth day of my Handship, and I did the necessary chores and freed the beasties to roam and et. I reset the 'lectro-traps to keep them within the lon' vale that centered on the Spiretown, and to warn me of aught that tried to enter. Then I went down once 'gain to the studiants' camp and checked the commset; but I found jus' a dozen voices still speakin' there, and all were sad and mad with the way the war, it was goin'. The Knack' 'tack was stompin' the men and their towns into the ground, bit by bit.

But the grid was yet live, and that was a sign for me that the good fight was still bein' fought—by some-uns somewheres. I wanted to help, but what could I do? My ownsome death wouldn't have mattered, jus' one 'mongst the many.

I needed to know what the caves in the Rock-Hill were truly like, and so I spent my lighted hours, one by un, look-seein' into each, as far back as I could safely go. Some seemed raw and rough and narrow, and those, I knew, I could never use. Some looked

polished, though, as if man or somethin' else had cut their way through the ragged bits on each side, makin' rooms from what had jus' been holes in the ground. I could store a great many thin's in the caves, includin' the beasties, but not for lon', I thought. Nothin' for them to et, and not much to drink neither.

I was pure-like tuckered out by the time I finished, but at least I saw all that was there to see—and it would be the end of me, I thought to myself, and the end would not be lon' in comin' too, if I holed up in that there place. Yet, what choice did I have, truth be told? Naught else was secure 'nough, save maybe for the Town of the not-men.

CHAPTER SIX
"What Do You Do Here, Little One?"

On my fifth Handday, I went down to the Spiretown of the Old-uns, which I didn't really want to do; but I knew that I had to know if any hope could be found there in that strange and empty place.

I've told you, Meester, of my 'foretimes trips to that ruin, when I was a young-un, and how I would leave the place each time the suns went down, 'cause no-un spends the darklin' hours there—wellaway, save for this one time.

When I was close to twelvish in age, I came one day to that Town, and I thought that I saw in my mind's eye some view of what its olden days had been. The ones here, the not-people, had been thin, furry folk 'bout twenty or twenty-five hands high, with lon' limbs and lon'er finners, and dark, leathery faces like the tanned hide of a bokelope, cracked about the neck and eyes and mouth. They went 'bout their bus'ness back and forth, back and forth, doin' I know not what, goin' in and out of those rooms of theirs, whistlin' to each other in their high-pitched birdy speech.

This was all my 'maginin', see, or at least I thought 'twas way back then.

So, on that day I dreamt and dreamt and dreamt whilst walkin' from place to place therein, and when I woke once more to my ownsome self, it was nigh unto darkish night, and I feared down to my very bones that I would see the bogies comin' out of the houses of the lon'-dead, comin' after *me*!—for that's what folks had said 'bout this place, from the early-early times that I could 'member.

The houses of the not-people were 'lumined in a beauteous pale bluish light that waxed and waned like the pulsin' of a heart. I wondered at all the strange thin's that I saw, but I couldn't move, so scared was I.

At lon' last, one of those not-uns came o'er to me, looked down at my tremblin' body with its narrow eyes, and spoke somethin' in its whistly speech—but I understood nothin' of what it said. Then it reached out one of its six finners, which were half 'gain lon' as ours, and touched me on my head—I could feel it pressin' 'gainst my skin!—and spoke once more.

"What do you do here, little one?" I could ken what it said, but only in my mind!

"I...I...." But I couldn't speak more than a word, for what could I say to one such as this?

But it spoke to my heart as if I were a growner, and answered that which I would have asked, if I could.

"There is no word in your tongue for what this place is," it said. "I see in your thoughts that you have sites that honor the departed members of your species. You

may think of this spot as one of those memorials, if you wish, though it is not quite the same thing.

"And now, I think, you should return home. You may not speak of this to anyone."

And it touched me once more, just 'bove my eyes, and I felt the brush of sleep come o'er me then; and when I woke, the suns were shinin', and what I'd seen seemed to me a distant dream.

What's that you ask, Meester? You want to know: how is it that can I tell you of this thin' now?

I can't answer that without tellin' you the rest of the tale, so you must wait for the end whene'er it comes, as 'twill in good time. But for now, I think I've talked quite 'nough 'bout such-like. I must ets and poops and takes my rest 'gain.

See, I's still a growin' Hand, if you pretty-please.

PART TWO
THE SPACER BASE

CHAPTER SEVEN
"Are You OK, Rabbs?"

I don't think that Spacer Haillon liked what I said to him, but I was growin' weary of this game—and it seemed to me, it did, that for him and for the others here, I was no more than a gin from which they hoped to shake some fruitful seeds. I didn't like Base Ell-Eks-Vee-Eye, whate'er that was, I didn't like this-here bare rock, and I didn't like these folks o'ermuch neither.

I jus' wanted to go home 'gain, and see my Dads and bro's and Hands and stock, but my Stead was now a wreck with no large life left, as well I knew. (The Knack's didn't bother with any little-uns.) What might come of the Chorest-Grant and Chorest-Stead, I could not foresee, and that made me the saddest of all the folks in this place.

Maybe Billieboy my bro' yet lived—they couldn't or wouldn't say this unto me—but 'twould never be the same, none of it, and I would always be sad, I could see that truthiness now full well. Growners say that young-uns have no feelin's nor brains, but we 'vision thin's jus' fine, we do—and as for me, I've seen too, too much, I think, in my bare fifteen years.

I went to Caf'teria to git me some grub, but it was all this mushy stuff and tasteless tripe, nothin' really good in any of it, nothin' truly real, 'cause I could only et stuff that my belly could handle, that was fixed special-like jus' for me. They couldn't give me the fresh eats that they served to ev'ry-un else. I had a few bites anyways, sittin' at a bench a lon' 'ways from all the others, 'cause I didn't want to say nothin' to any of them. They were all Spacers and 'Gineers and such, not a rancher 'mongst them, and no Terr'fermers—no one like me at me. And none of them knew the ownsome *me*, not real-like.

"Are you OK, Rabbs?" Meez Burgs said, sittin' herself down next to me. She was a psych-tech who was s'posed to make me feel gay and bright and all goodie-goodies 'side. But I'd heared 'Ministrator Ginrak say that the Force had lifted jus' 257 Terr'fermers off our world since our war. 'Course, some of our boys were fightin' off-world 'gainst the Knack's, but no one seemed to know how many of them still lived.

I looked at her and said: "Good eats in the inside empire, Ma'am," and forced a spoonful of gray-and-green goop into my mouth. I kept on doin' this till she got the notion that I didn't want to talk with her, and went 'way.

The comm system began blarin', "Medics to Dock 36, medics to Dock 36!"—and I gazed at the big views-creen smeared on the far wall of the Caf'teria. A large SpaceForce vessel was matin' with one of the metal locks that pocked the outside of the rock; it was seared

'lon' one side with a zigzaggy blackish streak that broke through its skin here and there. I'd seen 'nough of these ships now to ken that this-un had been real, real lucky to make it back to Base 'gain.

I sighed: on and on it went, this damwar, with men and bugs fightin' and dyin'—and for what? The bugs ate men, the men ate bugs. It all came out the same in the end.

I 'member when they first brought me here, and Meester Ginrak had taken me to a viewroom some-wheres in the Base—the whole rock was hollowed out—and he showed me the dead bodies of the Knack's they'd found or kilt on other worlds. He wanted me to say whether these flavors of bugs were the samish as those I'd seen on Terr'ferme.

What diff'rence did it make? Maybe one was bigger, or one was smaller, or one had brown spots, or one had green fur, or one had bigger claws than 'nother. So damwhat? They were all the 'nemy, and they all needed killin', and damsoon too. The bugs didn't worry o'ermuch 'bout such-like, of that I was real sure. It was kill or be killed, Meester Human Person, and no pretty-please-Meester-I'll-be-good made no dam diff'rence to anythin' or anyone, no ways.

The only good Knack' was a dead Knack'.

CHAPTER EIGHT

"Some of Us Don't Wear Uniforms"

They left me 'lone for sev'ral days aftertimes, and I wandered through Base by my ownsome, lonesome self, wantin' most desperate-like to find somethin' good to do. But they gave me nothin', never, and I grew more and more sad as the days went by.

Fin'lly, Spacer Haillon found me in my roomette on Level Seven, Roshwald Sector, and said: "I have another session set for you tomorrow, Rabbs. I'm sorry about the delay, but as you know, we've had a tough week here.

"I do have some good news for you, however. We've located your brother, Sergeant Willims din Chorest, and have sent him a message on your behalf. You should hear back from him within a few months, if he's near an open comm station."

So Billieboy yet lived? So I still had a fam'ly? The Lord God had fin'lly given me somethin'! Then I wondered 'bout J. C. and e'en my Moms, whose fate I'd never truly known. I asked the Meester, but he said that they couldn't tell me whether they'd died or no—

and that the Forces might never be able to say for sure. I knew this in my own lonesome self, but I asked him anyways, foolish person that I was.

So, on the very next day, I met with Spacer Haillon in Room 113, with Meez Burgs sittin' to one side, and 'nother 'ficial of some sort, dressed all in black, plopped next to her.

"Ms. Rabbsono din Chorest," Meester said, "let me introduce you to Colonel Decim Nammbô. You already know Doctor Major Delfa Burgs."

"Why're they here?" I asked, wavin' my hand at the others. "'S'always been jus' me and thee, Meester."

"Doctor Burgs asked to be present at this session; she feels, I think, that she might help alleviate some of the natural tensions that can be generated by this sort of process."

"Didn't ask her to come," I said.

"I know," Haillon said, "but you haven't been your-self of late, and we think that the interview will go better if you have someone here whom you can confide in. A friend, if you will."

"She no friend of mine," I said.

"Rabbs," Meez Burgs said, "you know you don't mean that. You've had a rough time of it, worst than most, and you need...."

"What I needs," I said, 'most shoutin' the words at their funny faces, "is my Grant, my stick, my beasties, my Handship, my life. Nothin' else does I need."

"You know that's impossible," Spacer said.

"Still, that's what I wants." I turned to the blackish

one: "Who this-un then?"

"Colonel Nammbô represents the Knackers Investigative Team, or KIT. He's here to listen to your account of the alien city you found. He thinks it might be important to the furtherance of the war. He may interrupt you with a few questions as you speak."

"He may or he mayn't, so he chooses," I said.

"You got no uniform," I told the Colonel.

"Some of us don't wear uniforms," the dark man said. I could read nothin' on his pasty face, not a smile, not a frown, not nothin'! His hair was cut close to his head, so that his big ears, they stuck out like a batfly that I'd seen once on Homeworld. His nose was narrow, his lips were thin, his eyes as cold as those of the mini-reps that I'd once hunted and fried and et.

"Why do you need to hear what I say?" I asked.

"We need all the help we can get to fight the war against the Knackers," Nammbô said. "Maybe the artifacts left by this dead alien race on TerraFirma can give us an edge. You can tell us how to access their technology."

"Already I told this to yous. O'er and o'er 'gain I tells you the same thin'," I said. "The true truth be this: that I don't *knows* what happened back there on Terr'ferme—'cause that's what *we* call it!—and I don't *knows* whate'er 'twas that I did or didn't do.

"You peoples seem to think that I'm some bigsome hero-person or somethin', that I knows all these thin's that will win the great war for you. I's jus' a Hand, that's all. I don't know nothin' 'bout science or tech-

stuff or the Old-uns. 'Nothin',' I says, but you don't want to listen to what I says, do you? So I says it to you 'gain, Meester Militar: I knows nothin'!"

"Your mother would want you to help us, Rabbsono," the dark-haired man said.

"You know 'bout my Moms?" I asked. "You know somethin' true?" I was frantic. I screamed at him: *"You tell me what you know! You must! What happed to her?"*

I dived 'cross the top of the table, grabbin' at his blackish shirt with my two hands, and yellin' at him to tell me all, or go down to the deepest, darkest Hell-o. I think I got his surprise, 'cause he pushed his chair back so hard that it bent back and dumped his damass right on the floor.

Then Spacer Haillon grabbed my legs and pulled me back from the edge, holdin' me fast in my seat.

A shame 'tis to say, I started tearin' up then, I couldn't help my ownsome self. I put my head into my own finners, my eyes leakin' down a river, and lost my way into a sad, sad darkness.

"Moms," I said to myself, "Moms, oh, why did you go 'way?"

"Colonel, I don't think you should've have mentioned Ms. Chorest," Meez Burgs said. "You must realize, gentlemen, that we're dealing with a fifteen-year-old who's experienced a series of personal horrors that we can't possibly imagine. What you're doing here could destroy a very fragile ego-structure, one that in my professional opinion is on the verge of collapse.

"We need to end this session at once, and start over again later—or I won't be responsible for the results."

But I was so lost within my deep-feely sorrows, that heared no more of what happed there. Meez Burgs, she took me back to my room, and stayed with me till I could cry no more, and then put me to beddy-bye with some joy-juice.

CHAPTER NINE
"Some Days, I Can Scarcely Bear It"

That was a bad, bad time for me, and I can't tell any of yous how I passed through those days. All that filled my mind was the picture of my dear Moms, who might still hold breath somewheres out there, I knew not where.

Fin'lly, Meez Burgs, she brought me to this place on the Base, and sat me down in front of a screen, and said to me: "Rabbs!" She had to do this three or four times 'fore I kenned that she was there, e'en.

She grabbed my shoulders, and her eyes, they went soft with the feelin'.

"Rabbs!" she said 'gain. "Look!"

I looked, and 'twas the image of my Moms in the picture of the screen. I thought then that she lived, and the joy, it rushed right through my heart, stabbin' it with a dagger of hope.

"Moms!" I screamed.

But she didn't move none.

"Rabbs!" It was Meez Burgs talkin' at me 'gain, till I had to take my eyes off the stat thin' on the screen,

and turn to the psych.

"Look again, my poor Rabbs." She turned to the console and said, "Authorization, Doctor Delfa Burgs, Iota twelve, Zeta four-eight-six. Video report on Doctor Amas din Renfrost ast Chorest, KIT, TerraFirma Division."

My Moms' picture vanished, and a militar-man took her place.

"Report of Captain Osten Dompter, date 16 Benzo Ought-Seven, in re KIT Station TF-118, TerraFirma. Station destroyed, per standard practice, when breached by enemy. All personnel dead or missing. Team Leader Renfrost perished in final battle, together with…."

But I heared no more. Dads dead, and now Moms, and maybe J.C. too. Only Billieboy and me left to build the new Chorest-Grant. If Billieboy truly lived….

"Rabbs," Meez Burgs said, holdin' me 'gain, "she died fighting for you and for me. She spent her last year trying to help us to win this war. The others won't tell you this, but we're not doing so well out there, dear child. The Knackers are tearing us apart. Planet after planet has been destroyed, and while we've won small victories here and there, we can never seem to push them back.

"Your Moms left you and your brothers because she knew how desperately we needed her assistance. I know you think she ran off with another, but she didn't. Your father didn't approve of her leaving the ranch, but her skills were unique to Terr'ferme, and she had to choose. It was a hard choice to make, I know.

"I've never told you this, but I met her once when she visited this Base. She showed me your picture, and she worried most about you, the youngest of her children. She was very, very proud of you. She asked me several times if she'd done the right thing—and I couldn't answer her. If our roles had been reversed, I might have chosen to stay at home, if I'd had someone like you there.

"But that was her life, and this is mine, and she's gone now; and I have to find a way, like you, to live through the horrors that have filled both our lives.

"Can you do that, Rabbs?"

I was cryin' 'gain, for all the friends and fam'ly I'd lost—and would still lose, I knew. I looked up, and Meez Burgs, she was tearin' up too. She put her arms 'round me, and I 'round her, and she sobbed and I sobbed till I thought our very hearts would crack in twain.

Fin'lly, she said, gaspin' 'twixt her cries: "Some days, Rabbs, I can scarcely bear it."

"Me too," I told her. "Me too."

For that was as true as the truth e'er got.

PART THREE
THE KNACK' 'TACK

CHAPTER TEN
"Where Are You?"

"This is Recording Session 16-8825," Spacer Haillon said, "being the continuing account of Rabbsono din Chorest, a survivor of the Knacker massacres on planet Terr'ferme, a modified human female aged fifteen years, a working Hand on Chorest-Grant, and the fifth and youngest child of Chorest din Ravvs din Chorest, Steadholder of Pompeztin.

"Now, Rabbs, when we last met, you were telling us about the place you called Spiretown."

*　*　*　*　*　*　*

The Spiretown, I told Meester, 'cause that's what *we* call it. I don't know what the not-people call it, or if they e'en give it a name. They don't think much like us-uns.

On the fifth day of my Handship—so I spoke to you in the 'foretimes—I set out to see what I could in the place of the Old-uns, 'cause I knew that the Knack's, they'd be comin' real-soon-now, and I had to be ready for them, best as I could.

The suns were very shiny that day, for the season

was summerin' in southern Terr'ferme, and I knew that when Meez Gorgonio kissed her sis, Meez Ruby Griswold, high up in the sky, the air would build in heat.

The Old-uns had growed maybe fifteen or twenty of the great spire-thin's pokin' straight up out of the ground, and several more piled on top of those. But no-un had e'er been able to figure out what or why or how those places did anythin'. Folks jus' didn't know, e'en those from Versity School, or the Doc Mays's studiants of the world.

I didn't think to myself that I could ken better than any of yous, truly; I was jus' tryin' to find some way to fight the Knack's, and to keep my beasties safe-'n'-sound.

I noticed first-like, when I came down into the hollow of the town, that the Old-uns had planted these small spikes all 'round the edge of their place. Whyso? I wondered to myself.

I stopped near one 'bout as tallsome as my chest, and put my face real close to the rock, to see all the little lines and pocks thereon. Then I wrapt my right hand 'round the pointed top of that thin', and closed tight my eyes. When I blocked out the wind, the suns, and the Vale, it seemed to me that I could feel some kind of pulsin' heart deep down 'side. This was not like anythin' I'd touched 'foretimes.

Now, it's a truth to be told that metal ore, 'tis real scarce on the Terr'ferme World. Most-oft we buy those strips and bits from spacers, tradin' our clays and beefs

and such, as needs must be.

But this rock seemed metally to me, and most lively, like a hot rep-rat fan-dan-goin' 'cross the steamy sands of the Berdoo Sink. I wondered if this was sim'lar to the spire I'd seen up on the hill, that had the green power livin' within it.

I touched my stick to the blackish spear, and gave it a small jolt of the juice, but nothin' happed. Whate'er this had, 'twasn't 'lectro.

I heared a rustlin' to one side, and saw a coupla nibblers chompin' at their greens maybe three metes off, nigh onto the slanty row of sent'nel stones. Nibs were smallish, furry critters native to these parts, and they were good eatin', if you could catch one. My sight was part-hid by the curve of the line, so I made one quickish step back t'wards the caves, and zapped my stick at them when they ran to cover.

"Got one!" I said out loud when the nib, it rolled down into the grass. The other ran-ran-ran, and sank back into its hidey-hole. Wouldn't have kilt neither, though, if they'd had sense 'nough to hide themselves back of the spears.

I skinned and gutted the fat beast quick-like, and took it to the studiant camp, where I'd found a power stove yestereve. There I spitted it and got it roastin' on the grill, addin' a few herbs. I figured to make me a fresh, warm midday meal in an hour or so. I made a quick check of my beasties before settlin' down to my eats.

When I returned to the Spiretown, I looked first at

a place I 'membered well from my 'foretimes visits there, when I was a young-un. Three great black rocks rose right from the ground to make 'twixt their 'brace a large room. 'Twas lined 'round the sides with a shelf or bench, placed at the height of my head. It growed right out from the wall itself, seemin' one with the rock. So stron' was this shelf that I could pull myself up on it, with nary a crack nor a break to be seen. But I could not ken its use—and not for lack of tryin', neither.

And so it went, from house to house, if such they were, in that strange and empty town. Only one had a door, as I 'visioned such thin's. Some were big, some were small. Some were full open to the winds, others were crunched low and tight, too small for the Old-uns themselves to use. Some had rooms within rooms. One had a tunnel-thin' down at one end of the room, divin' 'neath the floor, but so far as I could send the light into that narrow hole, I could see nothin' save that 'twas smooth and round and very, very tight. I could not think to visit that place, not e'er, for the squeeze.

None of the spires had anythin' there that might fight the Knack's, leastwise that I could see. None would be better places to use than the caves I'd already found in the Rock-Hill.

To be sure, the Old-uns had put Baldy-Run Crik right through the center of town, carvin' a channel for it that dived most oft 'neath the earth, but rose up thrice to where a man or beast could free-like sip its nectar. That was one good thin'. Then too, I saw weeds and grass sproutin' here and there 'bout the place, but

not 'nough to feed my beasties for very lon'.

Also, one of the Old-un houses was filled with rows of large pots, topped with strange plants and fruits and flowers that I'd never seen the like 'fore. But I couldn't let my beasties et them, without knowin' what they were.

But of the not-humans, I saw no sign—not a shadow, not a ghost, not a murmur of sound.

"Where are you?" I yelled to the air, but all I got back was my voice echoin' o'er and o'er 'gain. "Where are you?" I heared, till the sound faded 'way, eaten up by the eerie whine of the wind scootin' through the stacks of dark stone.

I sighed: this was not helpin' my need, nosiree, so fin'lly I jus' quit my hoppin' 'bout, and whistled for Meez Lambo. I was walkin' out t'wards the edge of the Spiretown when I saw somethin' real odd-like. My beefer was waitin' for me, sure 'nough, but way out beyond the guard-spires.

I whistled 'gain, but Meez Lambo, she would not come 'nother step t'wards me; 'stead, she just danced and pranced 'round and 'round, like she had to pee real bad or somethin'.

Then I 'membered the nibbler I'd kilt earlier that day, and how it'd dashed into the open ground, 'stead of hidin' 'mongst the short pillars of stone.

So, I thought to myself, this line of dark-spears must help keep the critters out of the Spiretown. I went back 'side, and sure 'nough, I could find no sign within the place of the birds, bugs, or furries that should be there.

'Deed, I saw no life 't'all, save for me and the plants and the vanished ghosts of the lon'-dead not-men.

This was no place for me to hide, if I couldn't brin' my beefers and clorses back into the shelter of the city.

I went out to Meez Lambo, grabbed her halter, and tried to pull her past the sentry-spire. She jus' wouldn't go, not for nothin', and when I saw the fear come sproutin' in her eyes, like the weeds poppin' up in a field of pseud-wheat, I stopped myself and let her loose. She didn't ken anythin' but bein' 'fraid.

Then I pulled myself up into the saddle, and made my rounds 'gain. First thin's must come first with the beasties. But all was still well in the Vale, since I found no sign of Knack's or chasers, but only fat and plumped and happy beefers and clorses, munchin' on their endless meals.

CHAPTER ELEVEN
"Hello?"

That ev'nin', before the sister-suns had dashed their twin lights into the wine-dark sea, I checked the commlink once more, and found only four stations still sendin'. One jus' ran the same message o'er and o'er 'gain:

"Find shelter where'er you can. Hide your faces from the Knack's. Put ker'sene with a wick into a jar to make a big flame, and burn or boom the Knack's down. Keep 'way from towns and such. Flee to the steads. Be not taken by the bugs. Watch for the gas."

I listened to it twice or thrice, but then it cut itself off mid-trans, jus' like that. I checked the light on my stick, and it had now gone to a yellowish hue. The grid, it was fin'lly down! The end of all was nigh!

After fixin' myself a din-din of canned beefs and stewed greens, I rounded up my beasties, and got them situate back in their 'lectro-corral in front of the Big-Cave, as I was now callin' it.

I built myself a fire jus' out in front of the openin', where I'd dug myself a good, stron' pit of rocks, 'cause e'en when the days were hot-hot-hot in the

Blackmarkers, the nights, they could be coolish.

I linked my stick with the twin corrals—one made of the thinnish juice that I'd set way 'round the three openin's to the Vale, and one of the much stron'er stuff that I'd linked 'round my beasties. I'd also laid the lines for a third rin' to block up the hole itself, if needs there be. I could do no more right now.

I was dozin' with my back 'gainst the hard stone when my stick went beep-beep in my hand, and I woke up real-fast-like. Somethin' big had brushed 'gainst the distant post, somethin' had been zapped by the line. None of my far-spots had 'nough power to kill anythin' large, but they'd feel the nip, oh yes.

Real quiet-like, I dowsed my fire, gathered up my beasties, and led them back into the cave, settin' my traps 'fore leadin' poor Meez Lambo out 'gain. Another beep-beep came from my stick.

"They're tryin' 'gain," I whispered in my beefer's ear. "I gots to go see, Meezie, I gots to go see. And you, you're goin' to take me there. Never fear, I's as scared as you, my old friend."

The stick showed me how to go, of course, to where the Brisko-Crik came shootin' out into the Spiretown Vale. We rode a coupla kliks to the place, in the gaze of the second, fourth, fifth, and sixth moons, none of which 'mounted to a pot of beans by themselves, but gave jus' 'nough light t'gether to see our way clear.

I'd brought one of the clay shooters from the studiants camp with me, though I didn't think it'd do me much good, if the Knack's 'tacked. But I had to see the

thin' real-like for myself.

I kept Meez Lambo to a measured pace, so we didn't make much racket comin' up the trail; and as we reached closer to the place where the line had been touched, I heared some human voices speakin'.

"It's a zap-line, Gramps," one said. "Some-un has set it here, and not too lon' 'go, neither. Not 'nough juice in it to kill."

"Sure gives one a stim-stin', though," a second voice said. "I thought I'd been…hey, what's that?!"

They'd fin'lly heared me comin', for I'd made no push to hide myself, once I kenned these were real-peoples.

"Hello?" an older man said in a loud voice. "Who be you lurkin' out there in the darksome?"

"I's Rabbs din Chorest," I yelled back, "Hand of the Chorest-Grant. Joy and wisdom to you and yours."

There was a quiet then, and a whisperin' as they talked 'mongst themselves.

Fin'lly, the loud man said: "Joy and good harvest, Rabbs din Chorest. I be Safrans din Harmost, and these with me are my kinfolks and nighfolks. We claim hospice-right, and bow to the 'thority of your Grant."

Now, I'd heared of this Harmost-Stead; it was situate three or four grants to the west of Chorest-Land.

"What am I to do, Meez Lambo?" I whispered in my beefer's ear. "By custom and by law, I must honor them their rights. But how can I take 'sponsibility for menfolks and for beastiefolks, all onesome and the same?"

To Meester Safrans, I said: "I do grant thee thy rights. How many do you brin'?"

"With me as their Lead, thirteen do I count—children, women, and men—with three clorses, a bokelope, and two beefers."

I rode up to my 'lectro-fence, and saw their worrisome faces peerin' at me from out of the dark, like palish batflies jus' waitin' to sip your blood. They looked very thinsome and well-worn. Well, I could make m'lasses out of sweet-beets, if need there be.

I clicked my stick twice, and loosed the 'lectro-line coverin' the end of the Brisko-Vale.

"Enter with honor and with joy," I said.

And that is what they did.

CHAPTER TWELVE
"A Barely-Made Hand of Fifteen Years"

They'd hitched their twin beefers to wagons that they'd fashioned from tracks, and two of the clorses had been set to draggin' a half-ruined aerolift 'behind them—and not with much joy. When the grid had failed jus' 'fore the sister-suns had fled the comin' of the dark, they'd made do with what they could tote.

I reset the 'lectro-gate 'hind them, and then led them in a weary trek to my camp near the Big-Cave.

"Did you leave aught of food or sticks or shooters in the Vale, when the power, it did fail?" I asked their Lead.

"No," he said, "we scattered only the oldest clothes and goods 'pon the trail."

"Goodsome," I said. "Now, Meester, git your people settin' within' the ground, where they'll all be safe."

Now, yous be sayin' to yourselves, how strange this be, that a barely-made Hand of fifteen years was tellin' this graybeard Lead to do this and that and t'other—and so he moved, hop, hop, hop—but that was the way of thin's there, see, when a man, he claimed the

hospice right for hisself and for his kin. This was a hard thin' for anyone to do, to lay his head at the foot of 'nother, but what had to be, had to be, if lives were to be saved. I knew my Grant and I knew what had to be done there—and a made Hand was a Hand made, whate'er the age.

Ha, ha, I saw that smile crackin' up your faces, Meester Haillon and Meez Burgs; yessiree, we can make some mirth on Terr'ferme, e'en on the baddest of days.

But 'fore all was settled, I made my howdy-dos, and got their names and ranks and places all fixed deep within my heart-and-head, so I knew who was who and what was what in the days yet to come.

There was Illus din Delest ast Harmost, Missy of the House, of granny age; and Polycop din Harmost, eldest son, of middlin' age; and Ramfer din Harmost, younger son, of same age; and Onds din Chelem ast Harmost, Missy of Ramfer, of young middlin' age; and Foss din Harmost, a young-un girl of Ramfer and Onds; and Beant din Harmost, a young-un boy of Ramfer and Onds; and Avnir din Avnost, Hand, of young middlin' age; and Tibbs din Javeln ast Avnost, Hand and Missy to Avnir, of same age; and Ecors din Avnost, a babe-girl of Avnir and Tibbs; and Desp'r din Desp'r, a servant to House, of middlin' age; and Lasto dint Toupo, a servant to House, of young middlin' age. With the Lead, thirteen humans they numbered in all, plus the six beasties, all of them my 'sponsibility now. I could feel my head fit to burst all at once-like.

'Cause I knew that we had little time with which to work, so once the young-uns were settled down in their made-up beds of grass and blankies, I put the rest to fixin' the camp the way I saw it. Their food and goods I stored deep within the Big-Cave, where it was safe. My second corral was good 'enough to hold the six-beasts more that I put there for the night; I would look at thin's 'gain fresh-like with the dawn of the bright-day's suns.

When I'd done what I could that wear'some eve, I set them all down to sleep, for the half of the night that yet was unspent. But as for me, I could not rest, but sat there upright by the pit with the beasties, restin' the stick of my Handship in my lap, and thinkin', thinkin', thinkin' 'bout what I should do these next few days. I prayed to Meester Lord God Hisself, sayin' to His Lonesomeness: "Give me a sign"; but there was none that I could see, though p'raps the fault was with my sight, and not with His wisdom—and my wisdom was sore pressed that day.

Fin'lly, my eyes did close, and I knew naught more.

CHAPTER THIRTEEN
"We Cannot Help You!"

Meez Lambo woke me with a swipe of her warm tongue 'cross my face. 'Twas the Hour of the Early Dead, when Meez Griswold had yet to poke her rosy-rimmed face o'er the rim of the world, and Meester Night had yet to flee to his hidey-hole in the Big-Oceanside out west. We were still 'twixt and 'tween, I knew, but the Old Knacker, he was comin' down that pike real-soon-like. I frowned at my thinkin': maybe a day or two, no more, I figured.

No time there was to waste. I roused Seer Safrans, and told him of the many thin's I'd thought of durin' that lon' darkish night, and of what we had to do. I had more mouths to feed and water, so once the big-folks were stirrin', I set them to movin' all the foods and goods and such from the camp of the studiants to the safe-holes in the Cave. There was 'nough in those boxes, I knew, to feed all my cares, at least the two-legged-uns, for months.

I'd found a carton of plast-pipe stored in the old camp, and once the food had been stashed, I had my new Hands strin' that pipe from the sprin' that sprouted

deep within the Big-Cave up to the livin' areas on top. Then I told them to shift all the sticks and shooters and the 'lectro-charger from one place t'other, and also the commset.

But as for the beasties, there was nothin' that I could do for them. In the end, they would jus' serve our bellies, and naught much else neither. I had no grub to feed them once the Vale was closed to their munchin', and no way of gatherin' any.

Meez Lambo would be the last to go, I promised, but go she would, 'lon' with all the rest. No choice with all these other mouths to feed. I didn't have to like my choosin's to ken 'xactly what they were.

So, on the sixth day of my Handship, we worked and worked and worked, till all of us were nigh unto fallin' down dead with the fag-lag. When the twin suns went off to their beds, I stopped our totin', 'cause I didn't want to tell the bugs where we were or what we were doin' by shinin' our lights all o'er that Vale. 'Sides, I had other nibs to fry, so's to speak.

I gathered all those who used the sticks—mostly the Seer and his Hands—and t'gether we worked to knit a bigger-better 'lectro-web 'cross the end of the Cave. We had crates and crates of the sticks, all of them rich with the charge, with the 'lectro-maker to help restore their juice (one of the Hands knew how to make that work), and jus' a small patch we had to screen. We could hold them off for months, if need be, or so I thought, more fool was I.

Unless…but I didn't want to think 'bout that think.

None of the new-uns had wanted to see the Spiretown, though most of them knew somethin' of it. But that night, after suppin' on canned stew and veggies, I wandered back down to the hollow where the town was situate, and waited for the shadows to move. Somehow, I knew that this was the time and this was the place for the ghosts of the Old-uns to show themselves 'gain.

Sure 'nough, after an hour or so of just sittin' and starin' in the center of that empty place, I began driftin' 'way once more, and whilst I slept, I saw within the eye of my mind the lon', lanky limbs of the not-men, strollin' from place to place in their Town.

I watched and I watched, but none of them spied the human within their midst, till one of them tried to sit down right on me, and suddenly opened wide its bird-like eyes in fear or surprise.

"Who are you, and what do you do here?" it said in my mind.

"I wish to speak with the one I met before," I seemed to say back 'gain.

The tall Old-un said nothin' to me in return, but jus' headed straight to the First-Room, as I called it, the place that I had first seen in this Town. After a bit, 'nother one of the creatures stopped in front of me, and said: "So, you have returned."

"I have returned," I said, bowin' my head in respect. "I need your help."

"You are the first of your kind ever to seek our assistance. What is it you want, child?"

And then I told it my story, cuttin' out all the dirty bits, and smoothin' off the rough edges and wavy parts, so it wouldn't wander on for hours.

"So far as I can tell," I said, "Most of my kin have now been kilt by the Knack's. Soon the bugs'll be *here* as well. Truth to tell, I can hold them back for a time, but I cannot save my beasties, and my heart is very sad for that.

"You have such great powers. I ask you to lend them to me, that I can kill all the Knack's that come here, and save the rest of my peoples."

"We cannot help you," the Old-un said. "By our law, we do not kill animate beings, large or small. Not ever."

"But, if the Knack's were killin' *your* peoples…?"

"Child, they *did* kill our people," it said. "The Tribe, for so they call themselves, came to this world hundreds of thousands of your years ago, when they last swarmed through this part of the galaxy. We were caught unprepared, and we died by the millions.

"In the end, some few of us were saved by our scientists, who developed a transportation device that took us out of harm's way.

"That is why we visit these naked cities of ours here, to honor the dead from our past, whose memories we preserve in our songs.

"We come when *they* come, but they can touch us no longer. Our screens keep them from damaging the spires that we have created, or those who visit them. They will also protect you if you bring your people here."

"But not my beasties," I said.

"Not, not your beasts: the screens will keep them out."

"What 'bout somethin' to help me feed the flock?"

"We have such things, but under our law, cannot give you the technology," it said. "You must find your own way to survive, as we did."

"You can do nothin'? Without your help, we may all die."

"Then you will die. We all die in the end, child."

And then the Old-un turned its back on me and walked 'way, cold as a frosty morn in winter; and I woke once more to the chill air of the nightside.

I was shivverin' 'side too, with what I had to face. 'Cause I knew now that it was kill or be kilt, with nothin' else left to do. 'Twas us or them in the end.

CHAPTER FOURTEEN
"Did You See the Knack's?"

On the seventh day, the Lord God rested, or so the Great Book says. But on the seventh day of my Handship, the Knack's, they came down 'pon us.

We had worked all day, all of us who could lift a box, shiftin' goods from one camp to the other, movin' as many thin's as might help us in the war to come. 'Twould not be lon' now, I knew.

I was so tired, so utterly worn through by late-day, that I could scarcely lift my head. I found myself sleepin' durin' the short breaks we took for munchies, and then pushin' myself up a few minutes later, when some matter or other was brought to me. By the dawn of dusk on that evenin', I thought we'd done jus' 'bout all that a man could do for prep-time.

So, I ordered the pit to be flamed, and the good-stuff to be passed 'round, and the pots to be set on their roast, and we feasted that night as if there was no time left to live—as might well be true.

The young-uns were put to bed, but the rest of us sat 'round the fire, talkin' of the good-old-days we 'membered from our early-lives. Seer Safrans had

known my Dads in the 'fore-times, and when I asked, Meester talked of him as a young-un, when all his dreams, they had yet to be lived to their fullest, and how Dads and Moms had met, and what had become of my old-bro's, Corcer and Bennë. I saw them all in a diff'rent view than 'fore, as 'visioned through his olden eyes.

One by un, each of them went off to their beds, till jus' the Seer and me stayed fast.

"Did you e'er meet the Knack's yourself?" I fin'lly asked.

He sighed. "I saw the pics on the vidscreens, that first day, till the wires, they all went 'way. But when I heared that the bugs were movin' into the steads, I got my peoples out 'fore they came down 'pon us. I thought, jus' maybe, that somewheres out here was a place where they wouldn't find us. I thought wron', 'course."

"So oft 'tis."

"And you, Lead Rabbs, what 'bout yousome?"

I told him my story, of my seven-day Handship, and how I'd come to this place with my beasties, and seen the Old-uns in their Town.

"Well," was all he could say. "Wellaway."

The sadness was on us 'gain, 'cause we knew full-like that all of us-uns would die, in the end. All the bugs had to do was wait, and we would die jus' the same.

"Best that I take my leave," he fin'lly said, gruntin' as he rose from his place, and headed back t'wards the

Cave.

It was then that my stick beeped—jus' twice—and I knew that the bugs, they were here!

CHAPTER FIFTEEN
"Got One of Them Suckers"

I'd seen holos of the Knack's at the Study-Hall, when Teach, he'd told us young-uns the story of the Great War. They came from somewheres out in the Rimmish-Stars, so 'twas said (though no-un really knew), and they spread real-quick-like from world to world in leaps and hops, first goin' here, then goin' there, and not much in the ways that any man could trace. We'd been fightin' them for as lon' as I'd been livin'.

Yeah, yeah, I knows, Meester, that you ken all of this stuff already, but I needs to tell you what I knew way back then, 'fore my fight began, so you can see jus' where I started, and see jus' where I finished, and know what went on 'tween.

We called them Knack's or Knackers or bugs, and others said they were Crabs. In the flesh, they stood 'bout fifteen hands at the thickest, though some grew smaller, and some a tad larger, 'pendin' on their types. They had six of these castes: warrior, gatherer, tender, builder, mother, and male-drone. Most could spin webs like spidey-bugs, but they also had graspin' and cuttin'

claws on each of their ten or twelve feet, and could kick with them as well; and their fangs were death to any furry thin' they bit.

Men would whine and cry and yell, 'cause the bugs, they'd et any big thin' that moved, includin' humans; but no-un said "boo" when the 'nemy dead were chopped and fried and canned for us and our beasties to chew. I'd et some of the stuff myself—tasted like crustos from the sea.

Now, how did I know that the Knack's, they were fin'lly here, and not more of the runnin' humans? The beefers, that's why! The bugs stunk up the place like nothin' else on Terr'ferme, or so I'd been told, and the beefers, they could smell that stench from a lon' ways out with their big-nose.

I went o'er to Meez Lambo, and she told me what's what, that's for damsure. She was snortin' and pawin' and hoppin' the way the beasties do when somethin' scares the big-gees out of them. I led her and the rest of the pack back t'wards the Cave, and told the Hand standin' there to rouse his Seer, and to take my cares down to the rooms we'd made for them.

The strin' that I'd laid at the Vale-Gate was 'nough to tell me that somethin' big was out there, but it wouldn't hold anythin' large for o'erlon'. As soon as Seer Safrans came out, I told him to wake his peoples, and git ready to fight the Knack's—and off he went, shoutin' and yellin' to move-your-ass-folks. Didn't take lon' to git ev'ry-un to where they ought to be, nosiree.

Meantimes, that big bug out there—had to be a

fighter, sure 'nough—was pushin' and proddin' my 'lectro-fence, as I could read the signs on my stick. So, I amped up the juice, jus' 'nough to give the thin' a hello-how-ya-doin' jolt, and sudden-like I saw a flash of yellow light down t'wards Mentons-Vale, and heared a sizzly sound, like bork meat fryin' on the grill. I couldn't help but chucklin' at the thought of the Big Bad Bug losin' one of its hairy claws.

"Got one of them suckers, eh?" Seer Safrans said in my ear.

"Gave it a fair howdy-do, that's for sure," I said. Then I heared, very faint-like off in the distance, that grindin', put-put-put noise that they used for talkin' 'twixt themselves, and I knew that the Knack' was callin' on its comm to its brood-mates.

Well, we'd git no more action here until the other fighters came up, whene'er that was (I thought maybe t'morrow).

So I called the growners t'gether in front of the Big-Cave, and gave them the news, and said that half of them should go back to their beds, and half stay at their posts, jus' in case. And in four hours' time, we'd switch places once more, so ev'ry-un could git some sleep.

But I stayed out front, dozin' off and on through the night, till Meez Griswold, she showed her pretty face once more, and shook us all awake.

CHAPTER SIXTEEN
"I Hates You Too"

But first light brought no bugs to camp, so I went down into the Cave, saddled Meez Lambo, and rode out to see for myself what the damthin' was doin' out there. It was fixin' to be a hotter-than-the-sunshine-momma kind of day, the wispy clouds in the darkish-blue sky lyin' to ev'ry-un 'bout the near-time to come.

Still, if it hadn't been for the Knack's, I would've 'joyed this beaut of a morn, as me and the beastie followed the cheery crik down t'wards the Mentons-Vale. Not far from my strin', I pulled my beefer back slow, bein' real-careful-like with that bug lyin' some-wheres near. I let Meez Lambo sift the breezes with her nasal hairs, and she 'mediate-like pointed her head a bit to the left.

So, I eased us both in that way, brin'in' us step-by-step closer to our mortal 'nemy.

And there 'twas! It turned right quick to face me, and I saw a Knacker up close for the very first time!

And I realized somethin' in that first look at the bug, that it was more than jus' one of them creepy-crawlin' critters that we have on Terr'ferme, like the cookra-

chas that travel ev'rywheres with man. There was a 'telligence there, diff'rent from us, to be sure, but comin' right through in the line of reddish eyes. And the Knack' herself (they're all part of the female type, 'cept for the smallish males) was covered with fur on top, and also at the bottom of her legs; it made her look like she was sportin' a colored coat or somethin' (I saw later that the colors changed much-like from bug to bug).

She looked at me, and I looked at her, and then she startin' pawin' at the dirt with her hind legs, kickin' up the dust. "I hates you too," I said out loud, dippin' my stick in her d'rection. There was no way either of us could accept t'other, 'cause we were both fighters, and we knew this to be as true as true could be. She put-put-putted somethin' in her lin'o back at me. Then she turned 'way and settled back down on her nine legs— the tenth had been fried off halfway up the stump— showin' me all the dislike she had for my kind, save as feed for hers, and she wouldn't look at me no mores.

No point in waitin' for the daisies to sprout, I thought to myself. I wheeled Meez Lambo 'round, and headed back to our camp at the Big-Cave.

War would come to us in its own good time.

CHAPTER SEVENTEEN
"Fire!"

They came down 'pon us an hour after midday meal on the eighth day of my Handship, breakin' through my 'lectro-line like it wasn't there, and crabbin' their way t'wards my second corral a half hour later. We were sittin' there waitin' for them, like chasers plopped in front of a nibbler hole.

The largest of our shooters spouted hard-clay pellets a centim in diameter, and one of the Hands had synched them with the 'lectro-field I'd set 'round the Corral-Two, so we could fire through the fence. We had three of these, and they'd been mounted where they could sweep the field out in front of the Big-Cave. I figured that these couldn't much damage the critters, 'cept to break a few legs if they got close 'nough, but 'twas better than nothin', I s'pose—and we had lots of ammo.

Most of what we'd gathered were the sticks, which could be used t'gether to make the defense-fields, and also to jab at anythin' that broke through the fence. They could also zap the critters, but by their lonesome, they couldn't kill any big-uns like these; maybe ten of

them workin' at once might do somethin' serious-like, but that was a chancer if I e'er saw one. And how lon' would their power eke out in such a case?

We also had pots of ker'sene from the studiants camp to help power the charger, and to use in jars as throw-bombs—and the Knack's, by all accounts, would light up very nice-like 'deed if hit by one. But gittin' close 'nough to douse a bug was most like a death sentence for the tosser, I could see.

So, that's where we were when they came down 'pon our camp on that steamin' afternoon.

"Fire!" I yelled as they ran close to the 'lectro-line, and the three shooters let loose the baddest that they could flin'. One of the bugs went down, two or three of her legs busted out, twistin' and turnin' whilst she struggled to git up, and the others—I counted a dozen or maybe a baker's in their army—quickly carried her off.

From beyond our range, the Knack's flung some gas bombs at us, but the field zapped them into nothin'-at-alls. After tryin' such tricks for a half hour or so, and gittin' nowheres fast, the 'nemy backed off to a safe place, and thought 'bout their next trick.

"Ev'ry-un still good?" I shouted back to my crew, and I saw nods from one-and-all. Then I noticed some-thin' odd.

The bugs were settin' up some kind of gadget out on the field, and I got my range-viewer out to see what was what. One of their crawlers had arrived from Mentons-Vale, or maybe'd been dropped from above by a flyer,

and it was loaded with metal pieces and mechanical thin's. I could make no sense of it, but I saw the Lead Bug—the one that I'd injured with my fence—orderin' the others to disload the cart. Then they began puttin' the machine t'gether, whilst several others ran the tractor o'er to the Khols-Hill, and startin' diggin' rocks out of it and settin' them down on the empty bed.

This went on for some time, whilst the suns in their shinin' jus' got hotter and hotter with the heat-blaze; so I ordered some cold water brought up from down-below, and passed it 'round to my folks, with munchies, keepin' as many of them back in shade as I could, and still be safe.

I knew the Knack's wouldn't use their boom-booms on us, so lon' as they had any way of keepin' our flesh whole for their eats. That's why they'd tried the gas first, 'cause the stuff was good at killin' men but not cuttin' up their bodies. But what were they doin' out there now?

We fin'lly got the answer to my question an hour 'fore the sunny sisters sought out their beds. I heared a bang out there by the bugs, a whistlin' of the air as somethin' large flew our way, and then a great thud as the rock hit the face of the Hill jus' above and to the right of where we sat.

Bits of stone and brush and dirt scattered all 'bout us, givin' Hand Avnir a nasty slash on one arm. Only the bigger bits were stopped by the field. I ordered him and the others to withdraw under the hang of the Cave as the second missile was loosed. More sharp mites

shot ev'ry-which-way in front of us, some of them hittin' the shield-mounts.

On and on and on they came, poundin' on the Hill and on our fence and on our nerves, till we were fit to be crackin' with the tense-sense these rocks were makin'.

The dust rose up from the ground in front of the Big-Cave till I couldn't see much beyond the fence-line.

"I don't like this," I said to Seer Safrans. "Git our Hands ready for a fight, real-soon-now."

Another large missile hit the face 'bove us, jus' as the twins ducked 'hind the hills. "Gimme one of the shooters and two bombs," I said to no-un who was special, and then I crawled out through the dirt, keepin' my head and arms covered with burls, till I reached near the end of the 'lectro-space.

Sudden-like, I saw large thin's movin' out there, and yelled, "Fire, left and right," whilst I let go with my own hitter directly in front.

I heared a scream of pain as I tore up somethin' real fierce-like—I could feel the splat of stinkin' hot blood and bug-guts showerin' down 'round my head—but I jus' kept firin' at anythin' that moved, till I could see no more.

"Hold!" I yelled, and the shootin' ceased.

A moment later, an early ev'nin' breeze cleared 'way some of the dirt-fog, and I saw in the twilight the almost-dead body of a Knack' sprawled jus' outside the line. It was still twitchin' a bit, so I nailed a coupla

pellets right through the brain buried in its belly-parts—and that was one bug gone!

O'er on the right, 'nother-un was tryin' to crawl 'way, with half of its limbs shot off—I kilt it too, and that was two.

O'er on the left, a Knack' was dashin' t'wards the line, gittin' ready to heave a darter at me, and I clicked the light on a ker'sene boom, and tossed it right in its face, the liquid splashin' down its body as it lit up the young night. The darter broke loose and headed right at the line, but I plugged it with two shots. The big-bug screeched its death-cry as it fried there right 'fore me, writhin' somethin' fierce as it went down to buggy-Hell—and that was three gone!

The rest withdrew, leavin' their buds dead-in-bed on the field.

But as soon as I'd crawled back to the Hole, they started up their rock-falls 'gain, and these bang-bang-banged on our open door all through that lon', darkish night.

CHAPTER EIGHTEEN

"They're Comin'!"

The next morn, the ninth of my Handship, I called t'gether our peoples for a confab, and Hand Avnir—he who'd been hurt by the missile-bits—asked: "Can they do us any great harm with these thin's?"

"Not direct-like," I said. "But if this boomin' lasted many-many days, 'twould cover up the Cave-Hole, and block us all in, maybe for goodness-sake; but they want us for their eats, so that's no easy way for them.

"No, I think they want to kill our corral out there, which gives us the only way to strike back at them. If they send 'nough rocks o'erhead, some'll git through the net, and some'll damage the mounts, and some'll 'rupt the juice, till all goes down. Then what we have left for ourselves is jus' the entrance-field, and they can take their sweet-'n'-sour time in rootin' us out. That's my ken."

"Lead Rabbs is right," Seer Safrans said. "They can wait and wait and wait, and we can do nigh unto nothin' once we're blocked down into this place. But we have no good choices to make."

"What 'bout the Spiretown?" Missy Illus said.

"Yes, we could go there," I said, "if the bugs didn't take us on the way. But we have no food stored 'midst the spires, and no way of gittin' our beasties into the Town."

"They'll die anyways within' a seven-day or two," Hand Tibbs said, "or more the like, we'll have to kill them all for our eats, 'cause they can't survive lon' without feed."

"True is truth," I said. "So what would yous have me do?"

But no-un could think of anythin' other to say, from what I'd said o'er and o'er 'gain 'foretimes, and we were still talkin' when Lasto came runnin' down, and yelled, "They're comin'!"—and we all rushed up to our posts quick-time-like.

I'd set the corral-fence so that when the shootin' started up 'gain, it lit up the night, 'luminatin' all the ground 'round, and we were shootin' and yellin' and fightin' like mad devils, each and ev'ry-un. But Desp'r was hurt sore by a darter, 'fore he kilt it with a knife; and the Seer, he was o'ercome by the heat, which had barely let loose of us when the dark, it came up; and he had to be carried down to the sickbeds way below. Tibbs got herself a bug with a ker'sene-bomb, so that was four of them dead, out of twelvish. We'd seen no signs yet that the Knack's were sendin' more troops to help their buds.

Desp'r, he died the next day, 'spite all the meds we'd scarfed from the studiants camp; we had no doc with us to cure the big-hurts that war brin's to man and

beast. We burned his body in the corral, so that no bug could e'er call it eats.

* * * * * * *

So, this is how it went from my ninth to fifteenth day as a made Hand, till fin'lly, the 'lectro-fence died the death of a thousand hurts, and I had to pull ev'ry-un back into the Big-Cave. We kilt a fifth bug on the eleventh day, and lost Meester Ramfer on the four-teenth—and burnt him too before the corral slipt 'way from us. And we began to kill the beasties—no choice, real-like—one by un, eatin' the remains to honor their passin'.

Now we were truly holed up—but we had food, we had drink, we had each other, and the bugs could not break the web we'd put o'er the Cave-tunnel, or so I thought.

And then a great quiet descended 'pon us. The Knack's stopped their rock-heavin', and 'tacked no more. On the mornin' of the sixteenth day, I crept as far as I could t'wards the openin', and looked out onto the hottish plain (though it was still cool in the Big-Cave), to see what there was to see.

I counted seven of the buggers out there, includin' the Lead, who was still livin', and two others that were missin' a coupla limbs or claws. They were gathered 'round their crawler 'gain, doin' somethin' to it—but I couldn't tell what it was, e'en with my viewer focused tight.

They worked on that machine for 'nother day, slavin'

in the hot gaze of the suns, which didn't seem to bother them none, 'fore we got any notion of what they were tryin' to do.

I'd gone as far as I possibly could up to the entrance of the Cave, without breakin' the chain of the juice, and once 'gain was watchin' the 'nemy makin' somethin' that would win them (they thought) this mini-war of theirs, when the thin', it started movin'. A bug was sittin' up on top, makin' it go, and the cart came slowly t'wards me where I was standin', with the others trailin' on 'hind.

"Seer Safrans!" I whispered at the Hand standin' at my shoulder, and he quick-like brought the old man back up to the front.

"Look at that!" I said, when he stood 'side me.

He took my viewer and gave a lon', slow look-see at the sight. "What do they do?" he asked.

"I dunno," I said, takin' back the ranger. "They're not comin' here."

And sure 'nough, they were slowly movin' o'er to my right, till they vanished 'hind the rock face, and I could see them no more. All save their Lead, who stayed out in the suns where she could be seen—and where she could see me!

She garbled somethin' at me in their strange lin'o—I know not what—whilst lookin' straight t'wards the Cave, and then followed after the rest. 'Twas like she knew I was there, and wanted me to know that, fighter to fighter.

I left a guard posted there with the viewer, and then

went back to call my flock t'gether, and tell them what I knew—which was nothin' much, to be sure. We were still all gabbin' at each others an hour later when I heared a rumble, and the wall of the tunnel, it shook slightly, and some dust settled down from 'bove.

"What was that?" the Seer asked.

Then it happed 'gain, and then 'gain, and we fin'lly found the site of the noise on the left-hand wall of a tunnel 'way down-below. I looked at Meester Safrans, and he looked back at me.

"They're carvin' out a hole," I said, and his face went real-flat-like with the sadness.

This might be the end for us, I thought.

CHAPTER NINETEEN
"If Any of Us Live"

By listenin' real-close-like, we were able to judge that they'd picked a spot to dig somewheres deep down 'side our Cave, in the bottom thirdish of the tunnel.

"You think they can dig through?" Seer Safrans asked.

"Yeah, I thinks so," I said, much as I disliked facin' that fact. "And if they break open the rock, there's no place for us to go then."

"What are we goin' to do?" Missy Illus said.

Now, that was the problem, I thought to myself. I'd put us down there, and it was my 'sponsibility to git us all out 'gain. But I wasn't sure how.

"How much ker'sene do we have left?" I asked the Seer.

"Twenty, thirty jugs, maybe," he said.

I led them back up to the meetin' room in the top part of the Cave, and told them all 'bout my plan.

"But, you're talkin' 'bout blowin' out the Cave," Hand Avnir said.

"Jus' one small part of it," I said. "Jus' 'bove the place where the bugs'll come out.

"Now, this thin' carries a great risk for us. It'll cut our plast-pipe of water, so we'll have to fill as many jars as we can 'fore they come out—and e'en so, what we have won't last us for very lon' after.

"Also, if the blast we make tries to echo itself back up the tunnel t'wards us, we could be cooked by it—or e'en kilt. We want the force to go t'other way, if we can make it do that. We don't have much time, and we don't have many tools. But maybe we can fry a few buggers, if the luck be with us."

I asked for other notions, but no one had a better idea, so that was that, as they say. I and a couple of the Hands went back down deep into the Cave to find the right spot to burn, if one was there to be found.

I thought they'd break out about a quarter of the way from the bottom—that was where the noise was loudest now (and slowly growin' louder all the time). Some metes up from that spot, we found a place where the wall, it did squeeze and kink itself to the left and then to the right 'gain; also, the upper surface there seemed roughy and patchy.

"If we could blow this section and tumble it down on top of itself, they'd have a hard time diggin' through the rubble from down below," I said.

"I think it can be done," Hand Tibbs said, and took 'pon herself the 'rangin' of the thin'.

"Now," I said, "we need to find a place further up where we can block or part-block the way, to keep the gases stuck down below in the bug-tunnel."

We searched and we searched, till we found another

kink in the passage about halfway up from the bottom.

"This'll have to do," I said, and put a crew to work totin' the big-rocks down from further 'bove. "Be careful," I cautioned them. "Don't brin' down the walls."

Now, the only question was: would we have 'nough time to do ev'rythin'?

But e'en if all of it worked jus' as I saw it in my ownsome mind-eye, how much time would we *really* gain, truth be told? Not so much, I thought. Wellaway, I'd worry 'bout facin' the next thin' waitin' down that rocky road if I lived so lon' to travel it.

And so, from the sixteenth through the nineteenth day of my Handship we labored nigh without rest in the dust and the soil of the ground 'neath our feet, till we all were grimed and dirt-crusted with the grit of the earth, and worn down to our bones with the unendin' toil. We had to make our own tools, 'cause we had few diggers or other thin's of that sort from the studiants camp.

The young-uns, they filled ev'ry up glass and ev'ry jar that was empty with the precious awa, and the rest of us dug and pried and moved the rocks 'round and 'round, tryin' to make the blockage stron'. Made no diff'rence 'twas night or day: 'twas all the same to us.

And all this time, the Knackery noises, they jus' got louder and louder, whilst they cut through the rock from the cave next to ours.

Fin'lly, I thought that we could chance no more.

"We'll block the tunnel up 'bove," I said, "but one

of us will have to stay down under to light that torch. That-un shall be me."

"No!" Seer Safrans said, lookin' 'round at all the weary, worried eyes starin' at him. "No! We need you, Lead Rabbs, and if you die, none of us will live to see 'nother day. No, I'm the eldest, and it's my choice. *I* will do this thin'."

"No!" Missy Illus said. "You have fam'ly here, husband. You cannot jus' leave them go, this way and that. I won't let you."

"Let me," the Servant Lasto said, speakin' soft-like from the back. "I have no one here who cares for me. Let me take the glory of this death. Then some-un will 'member me in the far-times to come."

"If *any* of us live," Missy Onds said.

"You *will* live," Lasto said. "I knows it. And I knows that Lead Rabbs will brin' us through this trek to t'other side."

Fin'lly, I had to agree, 'cause she was right, and I gave her that word; and her face, it lit up like the suns edgin' o'er the Blackmarkers at the dawn of day.

"I can do this," she said.

That ev'nin', we made a feast for ourselves to honor her death-to-come, and san' some son's and told some stories of the 'foretimes (bein' not so lon' ago), when the harvests were good and the beasties were plump, and the livin', it was jus' real-fine—only we didn't ken that truth so much back then.

All of us, I think, wanted to go back to those days; and all of us knew that they would never come 'gain,

leastwise not for us, not on Terr'ferme.

Still, we ate and we drank and we smiled, e'en, for a few hours, and put aside the cares yet to come; for what else, really, did we have to do in that time of death? We could have cried our ill-fortune, and said, "Woe is to me," o'er and o'er 'gain, but we were better folks than that.

Few we might be now, but we would never give up.

CHAPTER TWENTY
"What Do You Suggest?"

On the mornin' of the twentieth day since I'd been made Hand, the Knack's broke through the tunnel wall. We sealed Meez Lasto down below, and ran back up the way, as fast as our legs would churn, seekin' out the hidey-holes that we'd made for ourselves in the big-rooms.

But nothin' happed, not at first, and I began to wonder whether aught had gone foul in the lower works. Maybe the bugs had moved faster than I had thought, or maybe Lasto couldn't light the match, or maybe.... A thousand thoughts rushed through my mind.

I think what really happed, though, was simpler than that. The 'nemy was worried when they found no-uns down there at the place they cut through, and so they moved more slowly than they'd planned, and made wide the cut they'd started, 'fore tryin' to move up the line.

And then, when they fin'lly saw Lasto jus' sittin' there on a rock, waitin' for them, they must have wondered 'gain, 'cause none of this made sense.

The ground, it rolled back and forth and up and

down when the fire, it was lit, jus' like a grand quakin' of the earth; and we felt the whoosh of the air surgin' up from below, e'en with the block in the tunnel, and the temps rose up and up till we thought we all were goin' to bake right then and there, and the rumblin' down below lasted a very lon' time 'deed.

I think that the passage that the bugs cut, and part of their cave, fell down on them with all the rest. They wouldn't be comin' up that way 'gain, that was for damsure.

I managed to crawl myself out to the entrance of the Big-Cave, and use my spy-piece to see what was movin' out there. Smoke was oozin' from their hole next door, mixin' with the dust from our place. At last, when the air cleared 'way, I saw a few bugs scratch themselves out onto the field of play—one, two, three—and that was all! We'd kilt four more, and the ones that were left were all missin' legs and limbs and claws and such.

But we'd lost Meez Lasto, and I ached in my heart for all those whom I'd sent to their deaths. I could never brin' any of them back 'gain.

One of the Knack's slowly crabbed o'er to the old corral, and waved an arm at me, chitterin' its put-put-put lin'o. It was their Lead 'gain. I think she was castin' her curse at me, or somethin' near-like. I gave the double-finner back to her, jus' our little way of sayin', "Go stuff it, bug!"—and she knew what I meant, that I could tell.

Only one of us would survive this war, and I meant that to be me.

I went back to my folks, after postin' a guard up front, and then looked 'round at all their worried faces.

"We won this fight," I said, "but we haven't won the war. We have little water left, and they know this. Only a few of our beasts still live, and they're very weak-like. We have to do somethin' to change the balance of thin's, or the deaths of our friends will mean nothin' in the end."

"What do you suggest, Lead Rabbs?" Seer Safrans asked.

"We have but two choices that I does see," I said. "We can 'tack them—but they're still three of them out theres, and they have the gas-bombs if we move out from the Cave. We have nothin' to stop the gas other than the 'lectro-fence.

"Or, I cans call 'pon the Old-uns 'gain, and beg for their help."

"But you said that they wouldn't help you 'fore."

"'Tis true," I said. "Yet, I sees no other thin that we can do 'cept die, and I ain't ready yet to do that. How many beasties still live?"

"Five," Missy Illus said. "But none are doin' very well. We don't have the feed to keep them goin' lon'."

"I'll take Meez Lambo, my very ownsome beefer, and ride-like-Hell for the Spiretown, whilst you send out the other four, and use the shooters to make a ruckus and kick up some sand and dirt.

"We'll wait till the darkness slides o'er the world 'gain, and then send light-shoots right at the Knack-eyes, to blind them. Maybe I can git by the bugs 'midst

all the hustle out there, at least 'nough to reach the marker-spires. I don't think they can git through those."

"Neither can your beefer," Seer Safrans said.

"No," I said, but that was all I could say, for it was the simple truth.

I'd raised Meez Lambo from a calf, when she was just a few hands high, and she was more than a beastie to me, e'en more than some of the humans I knew.

But I had no choice: 'twas the only chance that I saw for us—and for myself. 'Twas us or them, and I would not go quiet-like to the dark whilst some-uns out there could still help us-uns. There had to be a way.

CHAPTER TWENTY-ONE
"All I Ask Is One Last Ride"

That night, after we'd all supped, I went down to the room where we housed the beasties, and found what was left of my poor Meez Lambo. Her hair was all stragglesome, and her sides were poked with bones, and her head, it hung down nigh to the ground. But then she saw me, for the first time in many, many days, and she jumped up, jus' then like the rouge range beefer of old, ready to go and do whate'er had to be done.

I stroked her and I brushed her out with care, puttin' her lon' hair back in place, 'cause I would not take her out to battle without her lookin' her best. I let her sip some of the precious awa and fed her a few sweets, all that I had left; and then I tied a bow on her brow, and I told her, I did: "We do a great thin' t'gether this day, Meezie, and then you can rest for all the times to come; and one day I will join you there, and we can romp through the Blackmarkers once 'gain, when the snows are gone and the grass grows green and we have no more cares in this world hereafter. All I ask from you is one last ride, and then, dear, dearest friend, I will spare you the pain of passin' through."

I think she understood some of what I said, or at least I hoped so. Her great brown eyes blinked once, twice, and then 'gain, and I knew the time had come 'pon us once more to do somethin' that I didn't want to do. As for me, I couldn't keep my eyes from leakin', and I wanted no-un to see me this way, weak-like and cryin' o'er a mere beastie. See, I jus' couldn't help myself.

But the time, it was wastin', and I needed to move on down that road, and so I led her up to the tunnel entrance, and there I saddled and mounted Meez Lambo, out of sight of any critter who might be lurkin' outside. Missy Onds then brought up the other four beasties, and had them ready to push out the door. We would have to drop the fence jus' for a moment to let us all through.

I counted down from five, and then yelled, "Now!"— and with a cracklin' sound, the 'lectro-field was spent. I jabbed Meez Lambo in the sides with my boots, and we were runnin' t'wards the Spiretown as fast as that starvin' creature could go, whilst the other beasties were peltin' this way and that throughout the old corral.

We'd caught the buggers, I thought, quite sudden-like, with only one standin' nearby, and the other two doin' somethin' o'er at the Knack' camp that had the crawler. Out of the edge of my eye, I saw the near-un jump a clorse and roll it o'er in the dust—but she wouldn't git much of them bones!

Meez Lambo was already breathin' real-hard-now, huffin' and puffin' without her max-stren'th to use, but goin' t'wards the old studiants camp as fast as I'd

e'er seen her run. I saw the Lead Knack' take out after us, in that sideways crabbish gait of theirs, but there was nothin' I could do but let this play wind on to its destined end.

I'd left the shooters with the others, so I had nothin' with me but my stick (and that wouldn't stop somethin' the size of the bug), and one ker'sene bomb.

I'd told Seer Safrans what he had to do if I didn't return. He didn't like it none—nor did I—but if we ran out of water, as we soon would, we would have no other choice but to put the others to sleep, and then burn the place down with the rest of the ker'sene, so that the bugs couldn't harvest the bodies. The last one would have to light the match.

And that would be the end of this game, if I couldn't find some other way to fix it. We'd give them nothin' to chaw.

Meez Lambo ran and ran and ran her guts right out, till she was covered with foam 'round her mouth and head, and was gaspin' deep, deep breaths with ev'ry stride she made—and still she wouldn't quit. On and on she ran, the Lead Knack' slowly gainin' 'hind us; I could hear the scrabblin' of her buggy-legs as she got nearer and nearer, but I didn't dare look back.

Jus' this side of the standin' stones of the Old-uns, my beefer's great heart fin'lly gave out, and she skidded head first into the dirt, throwin' me o'er the front of her, and knockin' the wind from my lungs as I hit the ground. I could hear the bug comin' up fast 'pon us.

Somehow the bomb-jug hadn't cracked, and I tried

to light it once-twice-thrice 'fore it fin'lly flamed, and then sent it on a weak arch—all that I could manage— that hit the back of Meez Lambo's dead body, settin' it afire with a whoosh.

The Lead Knack' skidded to a halt sudden-like, and had to rear back to 'void the heat, whilst I tried to roll myself o'er and o'er 'gain towards the line of the guard-spires protectin' the Old-uns' Town.

The great-bug then found herself once more, and hopped straight up in the air, jumpin' o'er the burnin' body of my beast. I jus' kept on rollin', not knowin' how far I had to go to be safe, and was stunned when the giant body of the critter slammed to the ground right 'hind me, stopped by the sizzle of an Old-un-field. I don't think she was more than a coupla metes from me then.

We stared right at each other, the hate fillin' the air 'tween us, but there was nothin' neither of us could do 'bout it. I was beyond her reach, and I had no weapons left that would harm the bug.

A force greater than either of us could wield had kept us from killin' one 'nother. Maybe there was a lesson in there somewheres for all of us-uns.

PART FOUR
THE OLD-UNS

CHAPTER TWENTY-TWO
"Why, Why, Why?"

I was weary beyond bein' tired-tired-tired at all this gabbin' and gawkin', and so I blurted out some hard words, without e'en thinkin' 'bout them: "This place, it's badder than anythin' I left 'hind. I'd rather go back to all that death and destroyin', than stay in this place any lon'er."

I put my face in my hands, for all the mem'ries of those days were comin' back at me now, and I couldn't rid my mind of any of them—of the dyin' and the hurtin' and the ravagin' of the land, and all those peoples under *my* care whom I'd failed, and the sad, sad end of my rouge range beefer, Meez Lambo—that was 'most-like the baddest feelin' of them all, or so it seemed to me, 'cause she couldn't do nothin' to save herself.

"Whyyyy?" I screamed at them all jus' as loud as I could. *"Why, why, why?"*

"I think we need to take a break," Doc Burgs said to the Spacer—and t'other far-watchers that I thought were always there, hidin' 'round in the back of thin's, keepin' their flitchy faces covered so I couldn't see. She

came o'er to me and put an arm 'round my shoulder.

"I needs to use the jane," I said. "And I wants some awa."

"What's she saying now?" Spacer Haillon asked.

"She has to use the facilities," Doc Burgs said, "and she would like some water, please."

"Oh." That's all he could brin' up from down there where his heart, 'twas s'posed to be, jus' an "Oh." These peoples: how could they live with themselves? Sometimes I thought they were as cold-cold as any dambug I e'er seen. At least the Knack's, they took care of their own.

So Meester, he shut down the 'corder, and said we'd "'journ," or whate'er that fancy-pancy word was, till the next morrow had come. After I used the 'cilities, Doc Burgs took me down to the Caf'teria on Level Three, and got me some din-din from the counter, though truly and truly, I had no belly 'nough left to et anythin' 't'all. I felt all sick and druzy 'side, kinda like when I used to have my monthlies, 'fore I got the shots back home.

"You've got to eat something, Rabbs," she said. Her face was all scrunched up with the worrisome lines of the growners. "You're just fading away from us. This, this god-awful testimony is making you relive everything that you wanted to forget."

"No!" I said, turnin' and grabbin' her shirt, and shakin' her a bit. "No, you don't understand, Meez Burgs! I don't wants to forget *any* of it! I don't wants to lose *any* of it. It's all that I've got left from my days

back on Terr'ferme—all that I still have of my fam'ly and my friends and my beasties. There's nothin' else now for me. Nothin'! Why should I lives when they've all died? Why?"

I was jus' eaten up with the rage and the big-sads and the knowin' that I couldn't save ev'ry-un that was my 'sponsibility. I couldn't et, I couldn't sleep, I couldn't go anywheres without 'memberin' of *all* of it, *all* the time. I felt like there was nothin' left but those bad-bad-thoughts, and no-un who cared anymores whether I lived or I died.

Meez Burgs, she didn't say nothin' 'bout any of that, but jus' put her arms 'round me and held me real-close, like my Moms used to do when I was a young-un, all snuggled up tight 'gainst the warmth of her bod; and I teared and teared for all the days that were gone, and for all those that might yet come, since I saw no way for me to walk through any of them 'gain, not with my head held high.

What was I to do? Oh, Great Lord Above, what e'er was I to do?

CHAPTER TWENTY-THREE
"Find a Way to Do It 'Gain"

"Gentlemen," Doc Burgs said, "I must insist that we keep these sessions to short stints that Rabbs can tolerate. If you don't follow my guide on this, I will have to file an official protest over the way this hearing has been conducted—and you know what that means."

A voice came out from the wall in front of me: "We don't want an inquiry, Major. All we're looking for, really, is any information we can use against the Knackers. Ms. Chorest is one of the very few individuals who's had an extended encounter with the enemy, and has lived to tell the tale. Once we've heard her story and asked our questions, she'll be turned over to you for whatever treatment you deem appropriate.

"Agreed?"

"Very well," she said, though I could tell she wasn't 't'all happy 'bout what he'd said. She couldn't do nothin' 'bout it, though, anymores than the rest of us-uns.

"Then let us proceed," Spacer Haillon said from my left.

* * * * * * *

The Lead bug and I stared at each other 'cross the invisible line that kept us 'part, but she couldn't reach me, and I had nothin' left that could hurt her. So fin'ly, I jus' turned my face 'way from her, pushed myself back up, and walked down into the Spiretown once more.

"Meester!" I yelled out as loud as I could to the cold, hard, black rocks, "Meester Speaker, I needs you!" I could hears my voice comin' right back at me, "...you, you, you," o'er and o'er 'gain.

Then sudden-like, my dream-state o'ercame me, so that I could see the shadow-folks wand'rin' their ways 'gain, and all of them, ev'ry-un that I could see, stopped and turned to look at me! Ev'ry-un heared me, and none of them liked havin' me there 't'all, disturbin' their peace. That gave me a thought.

"Meester!" I shouted 'gain. "Meester! You come to me right now, or I'll git so much noise goin' on here that none of yous will e'er want to come back to this place."

I pulled out my stick, and started hittin' it 'gainst one of the small spires made of thin rods, makin' a racket right out of Hell-o itself. "Bang! Bang! Bang! Bang!" went my stick, and then I began runnin' it up and down the sides. The Old-uns covered their ears with their hands, but still they heared ev'ry note of the merry music I made with my toy. "Bang! Bang! Bang!" I continued. "Meester!" I shouted as loud as I could, o'er and o'er and o'er.

"Enough!" the Speaker said, fin'lly comin' 'fore me.

I left my arm raised high.

"Help me," I said, "or I will make you sadder than you e'er knew was possible."

The not-man grew very green in its face, and pulled a short-stick out from 'neath its cloak, and was gittin' ready to wave it at me, when I said: "You can't harm 'nother bein'—you said so yourself. 'Gainst your laws or somethin'."

"Sending you away is not harming you," it said in my mind.

"How do you know that?" I asked. "You haven't given any time 't'all to knowin' us or our special ways. You look at us like *we* look at the nibblers out there, as jus' nothin's. You think you know better than any of us—better than anyone, really. Yous are all badder e'en than the Knack's—at least they care 'bout us as feed, if nothin' else. You care not at all for anyones."

"We cannot give you the weapons you desire," it said. "So we cannot help you."

"I didn't ask for any shooters this time," I said. "Jus' your help to find some way for my peoples to live."

"We cannot give you advanced technology. As you say, it's contrary to our laws."

"I don't want your glitchy gadgets," I said. "I jus' want some way to save those folks hidin' in the Big-Cave 'fore they all die. Not *me*, mind, jus' them. Take *me* with you, if that's the price I have to pay. I'll do anythin', Meester, but give us a chancer."

"Anything that I could give you would violate our rule," it said. Its skin was now pocked with points of

greenish goo. I dunno what that meant.

"Think!" I said. "There has to be a way. Look at that Knack' out there waitin' for me. It came down on t'other side of the line. It couldn't kill me 'cause you prevented it from crossin' o'er. True?"

"Yes, that is true," the Old-un Speaker said.

"And *I* couldn't kill it 'cause I had no weapons with me. True?"

"Yes, that is true."

"So, there we were, two 'nemies stuck on either side of the screen that *you* made. We still hate each other, but we couldn't harm each other. True?"

"Yes, that is true."

"Find a way to do it 'gain!" I said. I sank down on my knees, not knowin' what else to do. "Please, Meester, *please*, find a way to do it 'gain without ruinin' your laws."

I looked up, jus' brief-like, and saw that all of the Old-uns had crowded close 'nough to hear what we were sayin' to each other. Somethin' had fin'lly got their notice, had fin'lly moved them to…I don't know what. I couldn't know what, 'cause I didn't think 't'all like them.

"I will try," the Speaker said at last, and I could hear its sadness and jus' plain oldness echoin' within my mind. I think that some of that passed on to me then, and maybe that's why I can't do thin's so well nowdays. "Wait here, please," it said.

Then it walked 'way, the not-men movin' 'side so it could pass through; but they all stayed with me, I

know not why, not sayin' nothin', but jus' watchin' and waitin'—jus' like me. I felt that they wanted to touch me, but none of them save the Speaker e'er had the guts to do so—and so I couldn't talk with them, mind to mind.

I found a seat on one of their hard, chillish benches, and watched the greenish lights movin' up and down those great pillars that they'd built, and it seemed to me that the pattern of them was diff'rent on this night, quicker and more, well, demandin'. But maybe I was jus' dreamin' 'gain.

Fin'lly, the Speaker came back to me, and said: "In the place you call First-Room, you will find a small jar of ointment on the shelf. Take it, and put one drop every three days on the center of your forehead—and on those of every person you wish to save."

"What is this stuff?" I asked.

"It's what your biologists would call a 'pheromone'," it said. "It will make the Tribe think that you're one of them, and even when their minds and sight tell them otherwise, they'll be unable to harm you.

"But—and this is very, very important, child— you must tell your people that they cannot make any aggressive moves toward the creatures, no matter what they do. If you try to harm them, it might break the spell, and they might attack you again. Just stay away from them as much as possible.

"Once they realize that they can't touch you, they'll leave you alone. You have enough of the ointment to last for 100 days, by which time all of the Tribe will be

gone from this world. Then you'll be safe.

"One other thing, Rabbs. *You* must promise us—and I will know if you're telling the truth, because of the link that you and I possess—*you* must promise never intentionally to harm another creature again, for the rest of your life. If you do, we'll come for you; and you'll spend the rest of your days on *our* world. Do you understand and agree?"

I had no choice, not then, and not e'er, really, so I said: "On my honor as a made Hand, I do swear ne'er to hurt 'nother critter or human e'er 'gain." I gulped very loudly, 'cause I wasn't sure what that meant for the rest of my days; but I had to do it, Dads, I had to do it.

I thought then of somethin' else. "I don't know if we have 'nough food left to live three full months here. Can you help us some more, Meester?"

The Old-un breathed out very huffy-puffy, and in spite of the serious-like nature of this night, I nearly laughed at it. It was, after all, such a *human* thin' to do.

"You saw the room of plants," it said. "The leaves and flowers—but not the stems—can safely be consumed by your people. They may not like the taste, but it will sustain them for as long as needed. Do *not* uproot any of the growths. They'll regenerate overnight if tended properly. Now, is that all?"

I reached o'er and hugged the not-man, and kissed it on the forehead. Somethin' passed 'twixt us once 'gain, but I know not what 'twas, e'en to this day. The Old-un felt to me like a large, coolish rep, with slightly

scalish skin.

"Enough," it said to me once more. But I sensed a note of pleasure there, jus' a tad, 'fore it pulled 'way.

"Go in peace, child, although I think your dreams will always be troubled. I'm truly sorry for that. If they get too awful to handle by yourself, call to me in your sleep, and I will try to help you again."

Then the Old-un turned and walked 'way, and its peoples all followed after it, one by un. They went into the Spire-room with the tunnel, and that was the last that I e'er saw of them.

But I went to the First-Room, and found the jar that it had said would be there, and when I opened it, I smelled the stink of the Knack's.

I put a drop at the center of my brow, sealed tight the lid, and then walked out of the Spiretown, doin' what had to be done to save my cares.

CHAPTER TWENTY-FOUR
"Do Nothin' in Response"

The 'nemy Lead was still waitin' for me at the entrance to the Town of the Old-uns, so I stowed my stick in the light harness hangin' o'er my left shoulder, and walked right t'wards the bug. In the end, you either did the thin' or you didn't, and I saw no point in sittin' there and watchin' the crops grow.

The Knack', she trembled 'bout on her nine good claws, and when she saw that I was goin' to step beyond the spire-line, she shifted and moved and hopped this way and that. So I slowed down my pace, not wantin' to push the thin' into a 'tack, and shuffled to a stop right in front of her big-bod.

Now, that bug, she didn't know what to do! This close, I could feel the thin's that I'd never noticed 'fore, 'cludin' the huff-huff-huff of her breathin', comin' through a line of holes that dotted the base of each side of her bod. She reached down a coupla lon' feelers, and touched me up and down, up and down my form, tryin' to ken what had happed here—and she couldn't figure it!

Her "hands" moved faster and faster, strokin' me

o'er and o'er 'gain, with her brain and row of ruby eyes tellin' her one thin', and her nose (where'er that was!) 'nother. I could have laughed if hadn't felt so much like cryin'.

Fin'lly, she stopped, and breathed out so hard that the wind whistled out of her in somethin' 'most-like a screech, and then she stepped back two paces, turned, and started walkin' up t'wards the bug camp.

I waited for a few minutes, and then slowly followed her on that lon', wear'some trek back to the Big-Cave, tryin' to use the light of the moons three, five, and seven to miss the nibbler holes that puckered the plain.

I was plumb tuckered out by then. 'Twas the midst of the night-time-hours, and I felt like I'd been climbin' that hill for the whole breadth of my life. What new chore, I asked myself, would the Lord God ask of me now? What new burden would I have to bear? What next would come? There was always somethin' comin' next.

The bug went her way and I went mine, and I fin'lly came nigh to the entrance of my Cave. I yelled to whoe'er was standin' guard: "Wake the Seer Safrans and brin' him to the door!"

I heared Hand Avnir answer me back, and then I jus' stood there waitin' till he came at last.

"What news?" he said, joltin' me 'wake, for I was sleepin' right where I stood.

I yawned. "Send Hand Avnir and any others who're there back to the safe rooms, and then you yourself will man this post till the sister-suns, they show their

pretty faces. Mind, no matter what you see or hear, do nothin' in response. *Nothin'*, do you ken? Only if the bugs kill me and 'tack the screen, can you use the shooters or the sticks to defend this place. Do not lower the 'lectro-fence lessen I say so." I yawned 'gain. I was jus' so damtired now. "And if I'm not back by the dawn of day, you take the Lead and do what you think best, 'cause I'll be gone and et by then."

"But…," he said.

"Jus' do what I say, Seer Safrans, please," I said. I didn't have the stren'th to argue with him.

"Yes, Lead Rabbs," he said. "I will do what you say."

I heared him order Hand Avnir back to the rooms down below, and then I turned to face the bug-camp near the crik. I took out my stick and left it on the ground, and started walkin' step by slow step t'wards the three Knack's that I could see in the dim light, not far from their crawler.

They looked to me like they were talkin', talkin' much-like 'mongst themselves. Well, I would give them somethin' more to say, that's for sure.

Sudden-like, the Lead Bug saw me comin' and gabbled somethin' at its buds. They came 'round to face me as I plodded real slow-like 'cross the dusty plain, showin' my hands to either side, so they knew that I had no sticks or shoots with me.

My woes, they lifted from me jus' then. 'Twas as if it didn't matter whether I lived or I died. I was doin' what I had to do to save my cares, those that still breathed, and if this cost me my ownsome life, well, that was the

price that I had to pay. I had no fears anymores.

Closer and closer I came to those critters who had ravaged my world. I no lon'er hated any of them. I just wanted them to go 'way and leave us be—the few who still survivaled. My feet, they dragged in the dust, but somehow I kept on movin'.

Fin'lly, I was there. The Lead bug was right in front of me, and the other two sat to either side. I could smell the sharp odor of them, not like anythin' on Terr'ferme. Slowly they shuffled t'wards me, till they were close 'nough to touch, and then they started strokin' my bod 'gain, tryin' to figure out, I think, what kind of Tribeswoman I was.

I puzzled them, that I could tell. One of them opened her jaws wide, and lowered them till they flanked me to either side. Then she closed the pinchers, jus' slightly, till they touched me at my shoulders. I stood as still as I could, not wantin' to cause her to pierce my skin, which would surely kill me, I knew.

Then she backed off, and they started talkin' to each other, back and forth, back and forth, not knowin' what to do with this strange critter that smelled jus' like them—but *wasn't* them. After a while, I yawned 'gain, which got their 'mediate 'tension, but when nothin' else happed, they fin'lly gave up, turned their backs on me, and hopped back o'er to their crawler. There the Lead Knack' picked up somethin' that had to be a comm, and spoke lon' and fast to the uplink.

Ha, I knew that one! They couldn't decide 'mongst themselves, so they had to find some-un higher up the

chain. I figured we'd have to do this all 'gain on the morrow.

They no lon'er seemed to care 'bout me, so I jus' turned 'round and started walkin' back 'cross the plain to the Big-Cave. When I got there, I told Seer Safrans, "Lower the fence," and then walked back into the place from which I'd been gone a thousand thousand years.

CHAPTER TWENTY-FIVE
"The Water Is Runnin' Out"

"Are you whole-some?" Seer Safrans asked, when I stumbled through the Cave entrance.

"I may have found a way," I said. "Wake the others, please, and brin' them to the Large-Room."

E'en though I was now stumbly-mumbly with lack of sleep, I had to tell them what had happed in the Spiretown, and what it might mean to them—and what they yet had to do.

So when all the growners and young-uns were sittin' back 'gainst the Cave wall, with one sentry left up top, I gave them the relatin' of my time in the place of the Old-uns, and what the Speaker had said and done. I heared the ooh's and ah's when I told them 'bout the ointment, and what it might do for us.

"But," I said, "This is not the end of it. I think the Knack's will send one of their command-bugs down to the Spiretown-Vale, real-soon-like, and we'll have to face these critters once more. Then, if they leave this place for good aftertimes, we'll know that we've won this partic'lar spat.

"In the meantimes, I'll give each of you a touch of

this goo, 'cause it seemed to work for me, and I'll tell you what the Speaker-Old-un said to me, that you may not use your sticks or shooters or anythin' else 'gainst the bugs, lessen we make them mad 'gain and they forget 'bout these meds. To keep this from happin', I want all of yous to stay within the Cave, till we know for sure that all of the critters are gone-gone-gone. I will deal with the Lead-bug, if'n she comes."

"Lead Rabbs, the water is runnin' out," Missy Illus said. "We have 'nough for maybe two days. Maybe."

"Spread it out as much as you can," I said. "Seer Safrans, tell Hand Avnir what I said here. Now, I must sleep."

But 'fore I did that, I had each of them come to me in turn, and I put a drop of the fluid that the Old-un had given me right in the middle of their foreheads, from the eldest to the youngest, and then had the Hand sent down to git his own, so that all were dosed, on this, my twentieth day as Hand.

Then I went and laid myself down 'gainst the wall, where I could feel the stren'th of the rock pushin' at my back, and slept till mid-morn of my twenty-first Handday, when the good Seer woke me up from the righteous sleep of the dead.

CHAPTER TWENTY-SIX
"What...You...Be?"

"Somethin's happin' out there," Seer Safrans said. "We need you, Lead Rabbs."

I had to blink a coupla times 'fore I could 'stir myself back into the land of the livin' men.

"Here," Missy Tibbs said, handin' me a cup of warm awa and some pseud-wheat munchies. I 'most refused the water, but then realized that I must have somethin' to git me goin' 'gain. Fin'lly, I shook off the rest of the foggies, and headed up-Cave to see what was what.

A bug flyer had landed on the field 'twixt the crik and our hole, and the fancy-Knack's that had ridden that lift down were crowdin' 'round, talkin' to our Lead bug.

"Release the fence," I ordered, and then stepped outside. I left my stick in the dirt as I slowly walked t'wards the critters.

One of them was bigger than the rest, and she bore the fanciest fur as well. They all were lookin' to her for the Big-Lead, so I headed in her d'rection, stoppin' a few metes in front of her.

I waited and I waited, but she jus' looked at me, and

then said somethin' in their put-put speech to one of her buds. At last she moved forward, reachin' down her twin feelers to stroke my bod up and down and 'round. I could tell that she was as puzzled as the old Lead bug had been on yesterday.

Then she straightened up 'gain, and spoke a quick command. One of the bugs handed her a small metal box with a yellow light shinin' from within. She held this thin' out in front of her, and then said somethin' that was made into Terr'ferme words by the comm.

"What...you...be?" it said.

I didn't know what to say back to her. If I said that I was human, she'd probably kill me—and the rest of my peoples. If I said that I was a bug, she wouldn't believe me, and she'd probably kill me. I had to think of somethin' that would work.

"What...you...be?" it said 'gain. My mind jus' went 'round and 'round, a vacant field of nothin'ness. What do you say to a Knack'?

Then she turned to the old Lead bug: "You say, brains it have. Why not it speak?"

"I's Rabbs of the Tribe Chorest," I blurted out.

Then she looked back at me once more. "We not this tribe know."

"We're a small Tribe," I said, "We jus' live here in this place. Diff'rent bods, same odor."

"Why bods different?" the Big-Bug asked.

"To et the food on this world," I said. "We had to change, or we would have wasted 'way. Our commlink with the Tribe was lost, and we could not fix it. All this

happed lon', lon' ago. Now we've changed so much that we can't e'en speak the Tribish-tongue. All we have left is the smell on our bods."

She thought 'bout that for a bit, and then said: "Very strange."

She then gabbled back and forth with the other bugs for a few moments, before fin'lly sayin': "But law, law is: odor of Tribe, member of Tribe. Commander cannot other say. You with me will come?"

"Oh, I do wish that I could," I said, "but I would soonest die if e'er I left this place. I must stay here, 'cause time of breedin', it comes soonest."

"Ah, that too we know. Then, may your way one be."

"And to you," I said, havin' no idea whate'er what she was sayin' to me.

Then the Commander spoke sharply to her soldiers, and they all started loadin' up the flyer, takin' with them the stores that they had at their camp, and the bug crawler.

Whilst this was happin', the old Lead bug, the Knack' of the Nine Legs, came o'er to me and picked up the comm unit, switchin' it back on.

"I Psydaysthesyskorysuntron. You I know. You I again see."

Then it flung the box down into the dirt, and followed its militar-Lead into the transport. I backed off as they began firin' their engines.

And then they were gone! At lon' last they were all gone!

The Knack's had fin'lly left the Spiretown-Vale!

I went o'er and picked up the bug comm unit. Maybe I would find some use for it at the end.

CHAPTER TWENTY-SEVEN
"They're Back!"

I was very careful-like at first. I would only let a few of my peoples out of the Big-Cave at one time, most-like to fetch awa and such, till I was sure that the Knack's, they had really gone. But we saw no more signs of them, and fin'lly, I let down the 'lectro-fence, and gave them their free-times 'gain.

Yet, still I made sure, that every three-day from Handday Twenty, I dosed my cares with the goo of the Old-uns, doin' it myself to make sure it was done right. I also put back the warnin' fences all 'round the Vale. See, I didn't trust the bugs, not then, not now. 'Deed, didn't trust much of anyones anymores, not e'en myself.

I gave to Hand Avnir and Missy Tibbs the task of makin' do with the plants of the not-men, down in the Spiretown, and when first they tried some of the thin's that growed therein, they made a bad, bad face and said, "Uh— too sour," or "Too bitter," or "Tastes like nothin' 't'all."

But, with spices from the studiants camp, and some lon' cookin' in the pots, they soon made the leaves and blooms at least et-able, and sometimes they were 'most

goodsome to the tongue. Least-wise, they were fresh and green, when all else we had was canned or packaged.

And this is how it went from the twenty-first to the eighty-eighth day of my Handship. As lon' as we had 'nough food, 'twas better, I thought, to stay where we were. We had the commlink that I'd taken from the Doc Mays's camp, but as lon' as the grid was down, no-un could talk to anyone, not nowheres. If the food ran out, we could think then 'bout findin' a stash in some other place.

But I 'membered what the Speaker Old-un had said to me, that the Knack's would all be gone from Terr'ferme in 100 days, so I had some hope that maybe we would be saved in the end. What else could I do but hope?

And then, on the eighty-ninth day, everythin' changed.

I was workin' down in the Cave when Hand Avnir came runnin' into the room, shoutin': "They're back! The bugs have returned!" And then my stick beeped twice, and I knew that what he said, it was true!

CHAPTER TWENTY-EIGHT
"Why Have You Returned?"

I ordered the Hand Avnir to gather the peoples t'gether and brin' them to the Cave. I grabbed the bug-comm-box and my stick, and rushed up to the entrance. Seer Safrans was already out front, yellin' to the others to run, run, run to safety. I got out my range-viewer, and turned it to where the Mentons-Vale began, which was where my lights were showin' as the breech-point.

I could see just one Knack' way off in the distance, staggerin' like it had drunk too much of the clorse-milk-brew, and movin' real slow-like, so very slow-like t'wards us.

Ev'ry-un was now 'side, and I told the Seer to set the fence 'gain once I was outside—and then I headed out 'cross our old Corral-Two.

I met with the critter jus' the other side of Baldy-Run-Crik. She had stopped there, and had let herself down to the ground, jus' waitin' for me. She was the old Lead-bug from 'foretimes, old Psyday, as I called her.

I stored my stick in its harness, and splashed through the icy-cold water of the run.

I switched on the bug-comm. "I thought all of yous had left," I said.

I could hear the air-tubes of the thin' breathin' heavy-like in and out, a billows that labored, it seemed to me, more than it e'er had 'fore.

"All gone," she said. "All but I from this place, now gone."

"Why have you returned?" I asked.

"Rabbs of Tribe-Chorest, this day mine to die. Here I come to die."

"What do you mean?" I said—but truth to be told, she didn't look at all very well. Her bright fur coat was tattered and faded, and she'd lost another claw off one leg, and one of her feelers looked frayed at the end.

"Order and law and rule there be," the bug Lead said. "Warrior caste I am. This world, this time I born be. No more after that can I live."

"You mean, you were made for this fight only, for jus' three or four months of life—and that's all?" I was stunned by her speech.

"Yes," Psyday said. "This day I die. You and I, warriors be. Here where I fought, here where I die— my choice to die. You of same Tribe-odor, you my life will take."

"Jus' a minute," I said. "You and I are 'nemies sworn. Why me? Why not one of your ownsome buds?"

"Hard for me to say," the Knack' said, her breathin' comin' slower as the time passed. "Closer come."

I wasn't sure what she intended, whether she wanted to break the truce and kill me, or somethin' else that I

didn't ken.

When I failed to move, she said 'gain: "Closer come. Please, Rabbs of Tribe-Chorest. Time, no time."

I sighed and tried to put my fear 'neath me, though, truth to be told, I feared this great creature more than anythin' I'd e'er seen or met. Still, I couldn't refuse her dyin' wish.

So, I walked right within her embrace. She could hardly find the energy, I saw, to reach down with her feelers and jaws and touch me to each side of my head.

And then, quite sudden-like, I felt her thoughts down 'side, and all the joys of the hunt and the chase and the fight and the sisterhood and the womb of the Tribe, and I knew then what she wanted, and why she'd chosen to come *here*, 'stead of bein' remashed on the great bug transport ship.

This Knack' was a rebelly-sort, as much of one as she could be in a shared-'telligence-hive, and she'd tried to git her Lead to see that humans, they had brains; but no one at the end would listen to her. So, when her time came to die, as it comes to us-uns-and-all, she left the Tribe and came to the Spiretown-Vale 'stead.

"See!" she said. "See! Warrior to warrior we be. Me you beat, me you must re-plow. Promise me. Please."

Then I felt a great pity for this critter, in spite of what she and hers had done to my Stead; and I swore that I would do as she wanted me to.

An hour later, she died, and I had my peoples gather t'gether sticks and branches, and placed them 'round her great stinkin' carcass, and lit a bonfire to the war

'twixt the humans and the Knack's. 'T'would never end for me, I feared, but maybe some of the peoples would find a new way and a new place, somewheres out there 'midst the shiny stars.

PART FIVE
HOME

CHAPTER TWENTY-NINE
"I Saw What I Saw"

No other Knack's came to 'sturb our camp, so once 'gain I gave my peoples free rein to roam the Spiretown-Vale.

On the ninety-ninth day of my Handship, my stick beeped once, and my stat light switched from yellowish to the green light. The planetary grid was on 'gain!

We hauled out the commlink we'd taken from the studiants camp, and made contact with the Force ships orbitin' high 'bove.

The next day, my days as the Lead came to an end, when the Spacer flyer landed in the Vale, jus' on the spot where the bug lifter had been.

We were taken up to a great vessel, and I spent three days there before bein' moved to a destroyer, and brought to this base. And here I've lived e'er since.

Now you know what I know. Now you know that I have no secrets to hide. Yous say yous want to win this war? Find some way to talk to the bugs. That's what *I* say.

* * * * * * *

"Well, yes, we do thank you, Ms. Chorest, for your testimony here. Does anyone have any other questions?" the Spacer Haillon said.

"We've run some tests on the jar of ointment you gave us," came a blankish voice from the wall, "but it had deteriorated by the time we got it, and all we had left was a mess of dissociated chemicals. Do you have any other samples?"

"Well, sir," I said, "the Old-un Speaker gave jus' two thin's to me—that jug and the use of their plants."

"Well, we couldn't find any plants there either, or any sign of them. We've done a thorough search of the place you called Spiretown, and while it has some interesting features, it's completely inert energy-wise, has no tunnel-room, and none of the other curiosities you mentioned. There's also no trace of the people you called the Old Ones—no sign, really, that they ever existed. The container you gave us was taken from the camp of the late Doctor Kotts, the archeological director on the site. She also found nothing there, by the way."

"I saw what I saw," I said.

"Yes, and then that bug-communicator you gave us—the circuits inside were all melted. Again, it contained some interesting architecture, but nothing that we could retrieve.

"Now, clearly, you were attacked by the bugs, and you demonstrated great courage and fortitude in saving your people; but I really think that you made up a great deal of the rest of your story, Ms. Chorest.

Maybe you don't even realize it yourself. You've been under a great strain, after all, and you were certainly lucky to survive. But we can't find much of anything there to corroborate your tale."

"I saw what I saw," I repeated. "I was there, you weren't. You fancy men with fancy-pancy ways, you don't know nothin' 'bout nothin'. None of the folks with gadgets and weapons and brains lived to leave the Terr'ferme, jus' a fifteen-year-old Hand with nothin' but her wits to git her by. Been yous, you'd all be dead by now.

"I's had 'nough of these probin's and proddin's and pickin's to last me all my life-lon'. I won't says anymores to yous 'bout nothin'. Go sit your butts down on a spire; maybe you'll learn somethin' by it.

"Go 'way, all of yous! Leave me be!" I was shoutin' at them by then.

"Gentlemen, I think it's time that we ended these sessions, once and for all," Doc Burgs said. "Rabbs has been very cooperative with you, and I don't believe there's anything else to be gained by continuing to harass her with questions she can't answer. She's just a young woman, after all, who's been under a tremendous amount of stress. She's going to need a long time to recover."

"Very well," Spacer Haillon said. "This interrogation of Rabbsono din Chorest of the Planet TerraFirma, is now concluded, and our meeting is hereby adjourned."

CHAPTER THIRTY
"He's Alive?"

But I fainted dead 'way when I tried to leave that awful room, and when I woke, I was back in hospital 'gain, tubes runnin' into my arms, and my stren'th all gone to nothin'. My skin was the color of dead-ash.

"Rabbs, dear Rabbs, whatever shall we do with you?" It was Doc Burgs, sittin' there by my bed, and holdin' and rubbin' my hand; and she was cryin', I could see, though she tried much-like to smile. "You don't eat and drink, and then you collapse and nearly die."

"How...lon'?" I managed to gasp out.

"Six days," she said.

"They shouldn't have brought me back," I said, as thin's came slow-like to me 'gain. "I saw the Moms and Dads and bro's and Hands there, and I e'en saw the Lead bug. I saw all of those folks that I failed to keep on livin' back on Terr'ferme. So why does *I* have to live? *Why?*"

"Because you must," she said. "Because not to do so leaves us without any meaning. And we have to have meaning.

"Rabbs, I know what it's like to have no one. My

parents and sister were killed in a transport crash when I was six. They sent me to a home where orphans are raised by the state. It's no place for a child of any age. But one of the sisters took pity on me, and made sure that I got a good education and some guidance, and I found a path to take for myself.

"I still have no one—no husband, no children, no close friends. I enlisted in the service to 'help my fellow man,' as they called it, and all I've seen are heartache and body-ache, and men and women cut to pieces, both physically and psychologically. Well, my term's up soon, and I'm not opting for another one. I've seen too much as it is.

"But, the fact is, *you* still have someone! You still have family! A message came for you while you were unconscious."

"Billieboy?" I said, tryin' to sit up, and findin' myself so weak-like that I couldn't do so. "He's alive?"

"He was as of a few weeks ago. I've downloaded his vid into your console here. All you have to do is call it up. So, you see, there's some hope for you yet. Do you want to listen to it now?"

"Oh, yes, yes, yes, Meez Burgs!" I said. "Please let me see it!"

"I'll start it running, and then leave you to watch it in peace."

Then she spoke into the comm, givin' the access code, dimmed the lights slight-like, and left the room. A few moments later, the message appeared on the screen:

"Hi, sis!

"Now, don't be upset when you see this"—he was lyin' flat on his belly on a hospital bed, jus' like me—"I'm OK, really and truesome. I'm on a medvac ship haulin' me back to base. Jus' got shot-up a bit on that last drop, takin' out a bug fact'ry world. Can't tell you where, 'course. We really smashed them out there, but some of my buds, they didn't make it back this time.

"I heared the terrible news 'bout home a few weeks ago. Ev'rythin's gone, I guess, and ev'ryone we knew is kilt—everyone 'cept you, Rabbitface. It's jus' too awful to think 'bout, Chorest-Spread bein' burnt out and Moms and Dads dead, and all the Hands and stock. Do you know if they've found J.C.? They say we won't be able to go back home e'er 'gain; there'll be a quarantine on Terr'ferme for a hundert years.

"But I thank the Great Lord that you're still there. That's what keeps me goin', knowin' that I'll hear your sweet, sweet voice sin'in' 'gain somedays soon. I hears that you were this big hero or somethin' out at the Spiretown-Vale. 'Magine, my little sister, 'nother great fighter! Take good care of yourself, Rabbs: I don't know how I'd live if you were dead, too.

"Ha! You'll find this funny! I got shot in the keester! Never live that one down, eh? So, I's

waitin' to see if they let me loose, once I gits o'er this wound. I'll comes for you whene'er I can.

"I has to cut this short, they say. Somethin' 'bout keepin' the bandwidth clearish. We're goin' to git through this war, we are, and we're goin' to hug each other real-soon-like-now. You jus' keep that chin of yours pointin' t'wards the sky, and not the ground. That's an order, Private.

"This be Sergeant Willims din Chorest, Six-co, TF Brigade, Seventh Army, signin' off."

I let the tears trickle down my cheeks—I was doin' a lot of that these days—thinkin' that my big-bro' was still out there somewheres, was still goin' in spite of ev'rythin'. I sent a prayer to the Great Lord 'bove to brin' him home 'gain safe. Maybe I'd try to write somethin' back the other way in a day or two, when I had my wits more 'bout me than I did now.

Then the console beeped, and I said, "Yes?"

"Incoming message for Rabbsono din Chorest," it said.

"Please play vid."

"Authorization code required."

Wellaway, I had none. I beeped for the nurse, and asked her to fetch Doc Burgs 'gain, if she pleased. When the Doc appeared, she entered her password, and then the screen, it lit up. It showed the face of Seer Safrans din Harmost. He said:

"Joy and good harvest to you, Lead Rabbs.

"When they took you 'way so quick-like, none of us had had the chance to say much-much 'bout the Spiretown-times. They wouldn't tell us where you'd gone, or how to reach you, or e'en when you'd e'er return. They jus' wouldn't say nothin' 't'all 'bout you.

"Fin'lly, I sent a vidlink to the Actin' Planet 'Ministrator, a Spacer named Gen'ral Croque-Merder, and she said they were questionin' you 'bout what'd happed there, and that they might keep you locked up fore'er, if they didn't like what they heared.

"I said to her, I did, that that jus' wasn't right nor fair. I said that you had saved all of us-uns, that none of us-uns would have survivaled if you hadn't been there, which was only the truth; and that you risked your life for us-uns, and that you gave all that you had of yourself to keep us safe from the bugs.

"She said, 'What about those who died?'

"I said, 'All would have died without Lead Rabbs. How many children, women, and men did *you* save from Terr'ferme, Gen'ral? How many?'

"She went silent as the dead then, as well she should, 'cause she knows and I knows that they did *nothin'* for us till the Knack's, they did all leave.

"'Those who were kilt on Terr'ferme,' I said, 'cry out for justice. Let that Hand go: she was one of the onlies who did what she should have done there, what you *all* should have done. Let her go, or I will make a stink so big-big that the pols in Parl'ment will 'vestigate this mess right up and down and 'round.'

"Wellaway, she fin'lly said that she would do what she could, and I hears that you will now be freed from your jail, where'er you are (they still won't tell us-uns that). But they did say that I could send you a vid, and this I have now done.

"Lead Rabbs, I and my kin and my Hands all speak t'gether with one voice: we owe our lives to you and your Leadship. We can ne'er repay you for what you did for us-uns. We will always be in 'holdin' to you. If you needs anythin', send me or mine a vidlink, and we'll either come ourselves or send you help real-fast-like.

"They took us-uns out a lon' ways, and we were resettled on Planet Onzin. They gave us-uns a new Spread there and some stock with which to start o'er 'gain. But still we must take pills to et anythin' here, though they say they'll fix that too. We'll see.

"I heared that they're buildin' a monument to the Siege of the Spiretown-Vale. Some-un wants to make a vid out of it. The Force says

it'll brin' in more young-un militars for their war. I said that I wouldn't help them, and neither would any of mine. We've had 'nough of fightin' to last us all the rest of our days.

"Tell us where you are, and tell us where you're goin', so we can keep the link live always into the future.

"And—'Member Terr'ferme!"

Oh, I 'membered Terr'ferme all right! I 'membered it each and ev'ry night in my dreams, screamin' myself 'wake two-three-four times 'fore pseud-dawn, it did come. It got so bad that I didn't *want* to sleep, that I asked for pills to keep me up all through the lon'-night. But when Doc Burgs kenned what I was doin', she stopped that right soon 'nough.

'Stead, she gave me tranks to ease my rest, and when they bumped me out from hospital (another battle somewheres out there, and more wounded—always more wounded—brought back to base), I began to sleep ten-twelve-fourteen hours each day, stewed right up to the hairs on my head with those little blue pills.

Then I couldn't git them anymores, neither, and I went to her and begged her for some release from my pain. But she jus' wouldn't listen to me, wouldn't listen to me anymores.

So, I started walkin' 'round the halls of Levels One, Three, and Seven, which is all my pass would give me, in the hours of the early morn. Oft I would go to the great viewroom on Top One, where you could see some real-time visions of the ships comin' and goin'

from their ports—and wished then that I was goin' out with them.

'Cause I hated everythin' 'bout this place, everythin' and everyone, all 'cept Doc Burgs.

I liked her. I liked her a lot.

CHAPTER THIRTY-ONE
"When Do We Start?"

A few weeks later, Doc Burgs came to me in my roomette and said: "I have something to show you, Rabbs. Please get dressed and come with me."

I didn't really want to go, I didn't really want to do nothin' no mores, but she was the one who could git me off my butt, when no one else could.

"Have you eaten anything today? Did those pills help?"

She'd brought me some of the meds that were supposed to make reg'lar Earth food kinda et-able for me, but they didn't work when I first took them, and 'stead, I upchucked everythin'—and I told her so.

"I'm so sorry, Rabbs," she said. "Maybe we can get a gen-treatment for you. I do keep trying."

And she did, too, which made me feel that much badder. She was the only one here who cared 'bout me 't'all.

She led me down to Level Twenty-Five, where I'd never been 'fore, into the guts of the asteroid from which this base had been cut. Her pass 'lowed us access to most parts of the post that were hidden to me.

This area seemed like a hold of some kind, a large, central room with a highish ceilin', and partitions cuttin' off sections all 'round the rim.

"What is this place?" I asked.

"Humans are not the only victims of this war," she said. "Millions of animals have been killed or injured. Most cannot be healed. But some of the more valuable stock has been saved—and this facility is one of the places where they're treated, sorted out, and dispatched to the colonies that need them. I thought you'd like to see what goes on here."

I saw blue-coated vet-docs and -techs workin' in some of the stalls, and we walked o'er to one.

"This is Doctor Eugen," she said, 'troducin' me to a man of some fifty years, with darkish beard and hair, who had his arm all the way up 'side the rear of a huge beastie I'd never seen 'fore.

"You must be Rabbs," he said. "Major Burgs said she'd be bringing you by today."

"What are you doin'?" I asked.

"Palpitating the patient," he said. "You can have all the fancy equipment you want, but sometimes you just have to get down and dirty to figure out what's wrong."

I liked his 'tude, and said so. "What kind of critter is this?"

"You don't know?" he asked.

"She's from Terr'ferme," Doc Burgs said. "They were one of the early colonies settled in this region, and the stock there was cloned and adapted from Old Earth patterns."

"I remember," he said. "Well, we don't do it that way anymore. This is a horse. It's been genetically altered, yes, but in such a way that it can feed off the vegetation of almost any planet that we've settled in this cluster. It's also much hardier than the original version, and can survive extremes of temperature better, and even some drought conditions."

He pulled his arm out of that horse's butt with a pop, and cleaned it off.

"This is where we git our clorses from?" I said.

"Yes. Hard to believe, isn't it?"

"But they're so big! They're bigger e'en than the beefers."

"Would you like to touch it?" the vet asked.

"Could I?" I was 'whelmed by the idea.

"Sure," he said, and I very slowly walked o'er to the thin'. It was huge, more than twice the size of a clorse, though I could see some sims 'twixt the both of them. He took my right arm, and placed it jus' 'hind the great head, on its shoulder. Its hair was short and stiff, and the skin warmish. I could feel the pulse of its heart.

"Do you ride these thin's?"

"Some of them," he said. "They have to be trained to it, of course."

Some-un yelled from 'cross the floor: "Doc Eugen! Come quick!"

"Sorry, gotta go," he said, rushin' off to 'nother stall.

For two days, Doc Burgs took me 'round from room to room on Level Twenty-Five, showin' me the critters and the peoples takin' care of them. Some were sick,

some were hurt, some jus' needed a good lookin'-after.

"So many of them," I said, when we fin'lly broke for din-din on the second day.

"Too many," she said. "Some have to be killed to make way for others, because they have no place to go in the colony worlds. Not everyone there can afford the transportation costs, even when they desperately need the stock."

Then she took me up to the Caf'teria on Level Three. I was munchin' on some special eats that she'd got for me, but my belly still wasn't back to what it should be. It growled at me a coupla times, but I somehow I felt better than I had in many, many days. At least I could chaw on some greens for a change.

"Rabbs," she said. "I want to talk to you about something. Your friend Safrans's vid was leaked to the media, and there's been a huge outcry over your interrogation. The military has been forced to issue a statement saying that they're satisfied with the results of your interview, that they were just trying to get some help in winning the war, and that they're willing to release you immediately to any appropriate guardian, once the arrangements can be made. Since you won't legally be an adult for two more years, you can't be responsible under law for your own welfare.

"I'm sure that Seer Harmost would take you under his wing, if you wanted that—but you should know that literally thousands of individuals have now come forward, and said that they would be honored with you as part of their families. I don't even know how

you would begin to choose, but choose you must. The sooner that you're away from this god-awful place, the better."

"So many?" I said. "Why would they want me?"

"Only a handful of people survived on Terr'ferme, and most of those by accident. You and your friends were the only ones who fought the Knackers to a standstill. Some folks think that makes you a hero, and while that's true, I know that you just did what you thought was right and proper."

"'Twas no great thin' to kill bugs whilst my peoples and beasties, some of them did die," I said. "I jus' wanted them—wanted me—to live."

"I know, Rabbs," she said, "and I do understand. Well, there's another alternative. As I told you, my term in the service is ending soon, and I've already sent in my resignation, effective at the end of next month. I thought that I might buy some of the stock that you saw down below, with all the credits that I've saved, and get myself a spread out on one of the new worlds they're opening up, one that doesn't have too many people on it yet.

"The problem is, Rabbs, I'm a city girl, born and bred. I have no experience at all with farming or ranching. I'd need to have someone there that I could trust, someone who could tell me how to run the place, someone who'd be willing to accept the responsibility without my constant supervision. Do you know anyone like that?"

I jus' couldn't ken what she was sayin'. She and I,

t'gether on a new ranch? On our own place, jus' by our ownsomes?

"You would really want me there? Truly?" I whispered, not wantin' to hope o'ermuch. It had to be a mistake, sure 'nough.

"Yes, dear Rabbs, I very much want you there. I want you there forever and ever, if you can find a way to put up with me. I need the help, and I need the company, and I need your love. Please say yes!"

I thought to myself: fin'lly, somethin' good has come of all this mess. Fin'lly, fin'lly, maybe I could go home once 'gain.

Then somethin' else came to me. Or rather, three somethin's.

"What 'bout the eats? I can't et Earth foods."

"I'm going to get you a gen-treatment from the military that will enable your insides to handle ordinary vegetables and fruits and meats and dairy products. With all the bad publicity they've received recently, they'll have no choice but to do what I ask, and to pay for it too. It's about time."

"That's 'nother thin'," I said. "I made a promise to the Old-un Speaker that I wouldn't kill any critter e'er 'gain, and the word of a Hand is good. And I won't eat the meat neither, 'cause that would be the same thin'."

"That's your choice, Rabbs," she said. "Your decision and your choice, always."

"If I comes with you, would you promise me that when my bro' Billie comes back from the war, you'll give him a place on your Burgs-Grant, if he wants

that? He's the only kin I have left now."

"That's an easy one. I'd love to have any relative of yours as a Hand," she said. "And now, what do *you* say to my offer, Hand Rabbs?"

"When do we start, Lead Burgs?" I said.

"Please call me Delfa."

EPILOGUE

"I ' s   F e e l i n '   G o o d"

Planet Quetzalcoatl—a Year Later

I was sittin' one afternoon on the front porch of Stead-Burgs with Meez Delfa, sippin' some icy tea made from the flowers of one of the plants in our garden—growed from the seeds that I'd harvested from the Old-un pots in the Spiretown, and then hid in my stick. It had kind of a peppery taste to it, but I liked the heat mixed in with the coolness of the ice.

'Cross the road, I could sees our beeves gittin' fat on the daisies and grass, and a coupla horses loungin' in a pen off to one side. We also has somethin' they call hogs, and chickens, and sheep, and goats, and crops of wheat and barley and many other thin's as well. I still miss my rouge range beefer, but she couldn't have lived on the feed we grow in this place.

My tummy's somewhat better now, though still not the same as Meez Delfa's. I can et some of the thin's we grow, but not all. She says that, given 'nough time and more treatments, maybe I can come to those as well. We'll see.

The war, it goes on, but Billieboy my big-bro' was let go by the militar-folks, 'cause he couldn't sit still no more. Now, that was a day, let me tell you, when I saw my own kin once 'gain, after so lon' a time. We laughed and we cried and shouted and danced and told stories of the 'foretimes on Terr'ferme, and I hadn't felt better in many, many a day, let me tell you.

They say that we'll beat the bugs soon, but they been sayin' that for years. I didn't give them the ointment of the Old-uns that I'd kept hidden in my stick, 'cause they would have used it to kill, and I'd promised the not-man that I wouldn't do that. So I have it hid where I can find it 'gain, jus' in case.

I still don't trust the Knack's, and I don't trust the militars, and I don't trust the pols, and I don't trust much of anyones save my own folks here, and my dear Meez Delfa, who saved my sorry ass. Sometimes, now, I can e'en trust myself, but not always.

Billieboy and his new wife, Missy Damieta, will be comin' soon for din-din, so I'd best go sees jus' what Servant Sosia has in mind. Sometimes, she gits these really strange notions in that brain of hers, and I wants this meal to be a good-un.

"How're you feeling now, Rabbs?" Meez Delfa said, sippin' at her tea.

"I's feelin' good," I said, smilin' o'er at her.

And I meant it, ev'ry word.

AFTERWORD
"The Knack' Snack"

In the summer of 2010, I had an opportunity to help put together (with John Betancourt) a new series of Double novels and story collections for Wildside Press, loosely patterned after the old Ace Doubles mass market paperbacks of the 1950s-'70s, with the second half of each volume bound upside to the other, and with two separate covers decorating either side.

Within a month, I was able to issue contracts for twenty books, some of them comprised of pieces by one author, some with halves generated by two or more authors. Writers, it seemed, really liked the format.

Not long before, award-winning writer Ardath Mayhar had offered me a collection of three original short novels, comprising an historical saga of the South in the 1830s, a modern-day mystery novel, and a previously unpublished SF novella, *Slaughterhouse World*.

Originally, these tales were intended to form one 250-page book, but when the Doubles project appeared, I thought that I could pull the SF section out without compromising the integrity of the other sections—and the collection was thereupon issued as *Born Rebel and*

The Guns of Livingston Frost (Borgo Press, 2010).

I thought that *Slaughterhouse World* would make a great Doubles piece, both in size and theme, but the problem was finding an ideal mate for the opposite side. I had nothing in hand that was remotely like Ardath's story, and I didn't want to delay its publication indefinitely. I suggested to her that I try producing a complementary piece of my own, with her approval and review, and so *Knack' Attack* was born.

Since so many of Ardath's novels, both SF and modern, deal with young people facing personal crises in a rural setting, and since my friend Jill Vassilakos had long been urging me to try a YA book, I created Rabbs din Chorest as my first-person adolescent protagonist, part of a family of ranchers on the planet Terr'ferme, somewhere out in the "Cluster."

Her voice spoke to me immediately, and she was a joy to follow through her various adventures. I created for her a kind of folksy argot that I thought appropriate to the occasion; and I placed her in a situation where she had to mature "real-fast-like," to use her vernacular, when faced with a massive invasion of the "bugs," the vicious alien Knackers that Ardath had invented in *Slaughterhouse World*.

The story basically wrote itself from start to finish, and I was sorry indeed to see it end. As is often the case with my fiction, the novel deals with issues of communication, family, and questions regarding the ways in which we live our lives.

Rabbs is faced with a series of bad choices in her

life, but the choices still have to be made, and the consequences dealt with. This is why we also see her at some point *after* the invasion, when she's being grilled by the authorities regarding the appropriateness of her actions on Terr'ferme. *She* questions herself even more than her persecutors, wondering in her own mind if she could have done more—or saved more—if only....

If only....

We've all faced such things in our own lives, although, one hopes, not to the extent that Rabbs must, and we each fashion our own solutions that shape our characters as we grow and change.

I hope you enjoy my venture into Knacker-Land. Perhaps I'll go there again someday, real-soon-like.

Blessèd be.

—Rob Reginald
San Bernardino, California
24 September 2010

ABOUT THE AUTHOR

ROBERT REGINALD was born in Japan in the Year of the Rat, and lived in Turkey as a youth. He starting writing as a child, and penned his first book during his senior year in college. He's been infected with terminal logorrhea ever since, churning out more than twelve million words of professional fiction and nonfiction. He settled in Southern California in 1969, where he served as an academic librarian for 40 years. He currently edits the Borgo Press Imprint of Wildside Press, and has also penned more than 100 published books and 13,000 short pieces.

His recent works of fiction include four Nova Europa historical fantasy novels, *The Dark-Haired Man; or, The Hieromonk's Tale* (2004), *The Exiled Prince; or, The Archquisitor's Tale* (2004), *Quæstiones; or, The Protopresbyter's Tale* (2005), and *The Fourth Elephant's Egg; or, The Hypatomancer's Tale* (forthcoming); two science-fiction novels, *Invasion!: Earth vs. the Aliens* (2007; a trilogy comprising *The War of Two Worlds*, *Operation Crimson Storm*, and *The Martians Strike Back!*) and *Knack' Attack: A Tale of the Human-Knacker War* (2010); two Phantom

Detective mysteries, *The Phantom's Phantom* (2007) and *The Nasty Gnomes* (2008); a comic mystery, *The Paperback Show Murders* (2010); and three story collections, *Katydid & Other Critters: Tales of Fantasy and Mystery* (2001), *The Elder of Days: Tales of the Elders* (2010), and *The Judgment of the Gods and Other Verdicts of History* (2010).

Recent nonfiction works include an anthology, *Choice Words: The Borgo Press Book of Writers Writing About Writing* (2010); two collections, *Xenograffiti: Essays on Fantastic Literature* (1996 & 2005) and *Classics of Fantastic Literature; or, Les Épines Noires* (with Douglas Menville, 2005); two guides to the Deryni world, *Codex Derynianus I* and *II* (with Katherine Kurtz, 1998 & 2005); four histories, *San Quentin* (ed. with Bonnie Petry, 2005), *¡Viva California!: Seven Accounts of Life in Early California* (ed. with Mary Burgess, 2006), *The Eastern Orthodox Churches* (2005), and *The Coyote Chronicles: A Chronological History of California State University, San Bernardino, 1960-2010* (2010); a short autobiography, *Trilobite Dreams; or, The Autodidact's Tale* (2006); a cookbook, *Cal State Cooks* (ed. with Johnnie Ralph, 2006); and several bibliographies: *BP 300* (2007), *CSUSB Faculty Authors* (2006), *Murder in Retrospect* (with Jill Vassilakos, 2005), and *Draqualian Silk* (2010). In 1993 he received the Pilgrim Award from the Science Fiction Research Association. You can find him at:

http://www.millefleurs.tv